Stay Connected with Us!

Text **LOCKDOWN** to 22828 to stay up-to-date with new releases, sneak peaks, contests and more…

Like our page on Facebook:
Lock Down Publications

Join Lock Down Publications/The New Era Reading Group

Visit our website:
www.lockdownpublications.com

Follow us on Instagram:
Lock Down Publications

Email Us: We want to hear from you!

I0564746

Chapter 1

Bucks muttered a curse under his breath. He got her voicemail again for the tenth time. She had not texted him back at all. She hadn't even seen the text messages that he had been sending her since late afternoon. It was going on ten o'clock at night. This wasn't normal. He and his fiancée either talked on the phone, video chatted or texted each other damn near all day long.

He was worried. Too much was going on, his best friend had supposedly done Yvette super dirty, and he too had not been seen or heard from. Shit was getting crazy. Bucks had a really bad feeling in the pit of his stomach, and it had him feeling sick like it had Julie, before she knew that she was pregnant with their first child.

He tried calling Yvette. No answer, voicemail, inbox full. He cursed again. Now, he knew something was up. No way in hell did both of them go dark without leaving word about being unreachable.

"What the fuck is really goin' on?" he asked himself. Bucks went into his contacts and found the number to the man that Julie and Yvette saw as a father figure. He pressed "call" and waited for an answer.

"Go ahead," Lieutenant Michaels answered, after three rings.

"Mr. Michaels, have you heard from JuJu or Yvette?" Bucks asked.

"No. What's goin' on, Buck?"

Lock Down Publications and Ca$h
Presents

BAD B*TCHES WIT' GUNZ 3
No Talkin', Just Killin'

Written By
Christopher "Diesel" Hornezes

CHRISTOPHER "DIESEL" HORNEZES

Lock Down Publications
P.O. Box 944
Stockbridge, GA 30281
www.lockdownpublications.com

Like our page on Facebook: Lock Down Publications
www.facebook.com/lockdownpublications.ldp

"Sir, I have no clue, but neither been answerin', replyin' to text, emails. Real talk, I have a bad feelin' that's getting worse by the second."

"Your GPS beacon app werkin?"

"Yeah." Bucks quickly went into his GPS app. His iPhone was linked to Julie's, Yvette's and it was linked to T.G..'s, but his locator dot had disappeared more than a week ago. "Sir, neither of their locations are poppin' up!" Bucks told Michaels, looking at the screen. "Something is wrong! I can feel it! My girl is pregnant! She's vulnerable!"

He started panicking as thoughts of what all could happen to a pregnant police officer. The enemies that she and Yvette had, that definitely had the means and the balls to hurt them...or worse.

"Calm down, Bucks. Nothing good comes of worrying. Where are you at?" the lieutenant asked.

Bucks looked at the scene about a hundred feet away from him, waiting for him.

"Handlin' a lil' business. I can wrap it up and come to where you are."

"Call me when you're done. Sweep and mop the floor too, man." warned Michaels.

"Always," Bucks said, then he ended the call.

He turned around and stood facing where three of his guys had two men at their knees, hands tied behind their backs, faces swollen.

Inside a gargantuan garbage landfill in Zion, Illinois, Bucks had directed his homies to take the two there and wait for him. They had violated. They'd broken the number one rule of the streets—No Snitching.

Rumors of them getting arrested with heroin and coke that Bucks had supplied them with had come from reliable sources. Paperwork was provided. There was nothing left to say.

***

Bucks walked over to where he had parked his cocaine-white candy painted '85 SS Monte Carlo, decked all the way out, sitting up on chrome twenty-six-inch Ruccis. He grabbed the tool he planned to handle the two rats with and made his way back to where they were both so terrified that they both had shitted on themselves.

"B-B-Bucks! Come on, dog, please!" Giovanni cried, seeing the machete in Bucks' hand. "I'll do whatever you want, man! I swear to God!"

Next to the Salvadorian dope boy was Honcho, a half black, half Mexican coke boy that was as frail as a dope fiend. He sniffled and wept with his head bowed, petrified.

"You'll do whatever I want?" Bucks asked, taking a practice swing, like he was in the dugout.

"Yes, dog! Anything! On my momma!"

"Alright. This is what I want you do, Gio," Bucks said, then he wound up and swung the machete as hard as he could.

Half a scream escaped Giovanni's lips before the blade sliced through the middle of his head, severing it from his eyes and up, completely off.

Flip, GB, and Law watched as the top half of his skill and brain flew, landing about ten feet or so away. Giovanni fell face forward to the ground, the bottom half of his brain spilling out of his opened-up head.

"Die," Bucks said to the corpse, as blood spurted out of Giovanni's dome.

He turned to Honcho then. He saw the little dude trembling in fear. Bucks shook his head, then he wound up like Jackie Robinson and ended Honcho, letting him lie bleeding next to his accomplice.

Bucks looked up towards where the big tanker semi sat, behind where his homies stood. The driver saw Bucks give the thumbs up. The engine started. Flip, GB, and Law stepped aside. The tanker began backing up, until the rear spout was close enough to the bodies. Bucks, Flip, GB, and Law stood by and watched the stunning, milk-chocolate toned Dominican girl get out of the cab clad in a hoodie, skin-tight denim jeans and Timbs, with her hair in long auburn-colored twists.

Flip, GB, and Law couldn't believe the thick trucker chick wasn't into men. They knew her woman, nobody even thought about attempting to get at her, or Evelyn Valdez would be coming.

***

They watched Gloria open the valve at the rear of the truck, and unhooking a long hose, she started spraying the chemical that was inside the tank. In mere seconds, the industrial-strength acid began dissolving the corpses. The sound of floured chicken being dropped in hot grease filled the air. The men watched in amazement as Gloria made the bodies turn to puddles.

Bucks ran over to where the top of Giovanni's head and brain was. He picked them both up and tossed them into the acid, disappearing them.

"All good, papi?" Gloria asked Bucks after closing the valve.

"Yes, ma'am. Gratitude, mami," replied Bucks, with a head nod.

"Appreciate the help. Whenever you need me, I'll be around."

She gave him a smile that Flip, GB, and Law wished were directed at them. Without a word, Gloria put her hose up, then turned to head back and hop into her rig.

"Goddamn, shortie thick as fuck, nigga!" Flip said, after he and the others got eyefuls of phat round Dominican ass.

Bucks chuckled to himself, "Better not let Eve hear you oglin' her girl, Flip."

"Nigga, Eve can get it, too, Joe! On 'erythang!"

"I'm' out. Y'all keep me posted," Bucks said, not even close to having the desire to speak about his cocaine connect and friends' baby sister in that manner.

He dapped his guys up and went to hop in his Chevy. He push-started the beefed-up, supercharged LS7 engine under the hood and rolled off as Flip went to his Porsche truck, GB to his S-Class Benz and Law to his Jeep Trackhawk.

Gloria was turning her seventy-five-foot-long semi by the time Bucks reached the exit. She turned north on Green Bay Road. He turned to head south. He called his fiancée's lieutenant and was told where to meet. The call ended in seconds. Bucks groaned, hating how he swore he could feel that his woman and Yvette were in trouble, and needed help... now.

***

Face down ass up, Samantha moaned blissfully into the bedspread, while the thugged-out black man pounded her from the back. She was in her mid-forties, grew up in a Jewish family, whom had been very strict on who she interacted with. Shielding her from the world only made her want to see what she was missing. High school had been her playground and in college, she went wild. But to this day, she had never experienced the pleasure that a Black man could give her, until T.G. slid his throbbing ten-inch cock into her tight wet pussy.

T.G. gritted his teeth, cracking her hard, releasing his frustration on the white woman. He was angry, horny and desperate. She had him by the balls that she had previously sucked on before she had gotten up on all fours and demanded him to get up in it.

Her husband had stepped out for a while. Samantha was so sexually frustrated that she could give two shits if Webster found out that she was fucking a black, murdering dope boy.

All she cared about was the dick, and how good it felt up inside of her.

***

"Shit! Oh God! Oh God! Yes! Oh yes!" she cried out, burying her face in the sheets. T.G. cursed. He couldn't believe the old women had such bomb ass pussy but then again, she didn't even look old. To him she somewhat resembled the actress, Jennifer Aniston. Pretending that Samantha was the sexy blue-eyed *Friends* freak, T.G. lived out the fantasy that so many men likely had.

"Fuuuck!" Samantha cried as her body began trembling and shaking. "I'm g-gonna c-cum! Oh my God!" T.G. started going so fast that it sounded like a round of applause. He grabbed her hair, yanked her head back and made her cum so hard that she farted.

"Bitch! What the fuck!" he growled through clenched teeth. Samantha ignored him. She pulled his dick out of her, pushed him onto his back and hunching over him, she took his wet cock back into her mouth and started deep-throating him. T.G. groaned as the foxy brunette made his toes curl. Within a minute, he busted his nut. Samantha sucked and jerked him until he was empty, and her mouth was full.

She swallowed it all, then sat upright on her knees next to him, looking into his dark eyes. She found the tall dark and incredibly handsome man to be fascinating. She loved how neat he kept his haircut, and how toned his body was. Even with a broken rib, the pain virtually non-existent thanks to powerful pain meds, he delivered dick like a champ. She only wished that their age difference wouldn't be the thing that kept them from being more than acquaintances. As the thought crossed her mind, she remembered why he was in her presence in the first place. Being with him, for anything other than sexual fulfillment, was forbidden. And that to her was what made the sex even better.

***

"Why the fuck yo' ass always stare at me after we fuck, lady?" T.G. asked her. Samantha removed herself from the bed. Standing her naked and petite, five-foot-five still youthful frame up, she smiled again at T.G.

"You have work to do. Get to it," she told him.

T.G. made a tsking sound, shaking his head. "So, you just gon' put the pussy on a nigga, and swallow my nut, then shoo me back to doin' yo dirty work?"

"Yep. Unless you want to go to prison for fifty years minimum?" Samantha told him with a raised eyebrow. "Your choice, sir."

"What if I told yo' husband that you be suckin' my dick? How's that racist-ass bitch gon' take that?"

"I couldn't give a flying fuck! Be lucky that I let you fuck me! Now get your ass up and go do what the fuck you're told!"

Samantha grabbed her robe, put it on, then marched off to the door. Before she left out, she turned and looked at him.

"I remind you, do not play with me. That device on your leg does work."

T.G. looked down at what resembled an ankle monitor on his right ankle. Samantha's husband had forced it on him. It was explained that if he was non-compliant in any way at all, the press of a button on the key chain remote would activate the small toxin injection system inside of it. The venom from a Box jellyfish would be injected into him and within seconds, full-body paralysis would take effect, and T.G. was fucked.

He looked back up at her. She was smirking at him. After their eyes met, she turned and exited his make-shift room, leaving him with an insatiable desire to strangle her and watch her die.

***

After a quick shower, T.G. got dressed in jeans, a bullet-proof vest under his hoodie and Nike ACG boots. He grabbed the two Glock 17s Samantha supplied him with for his "workload," slapping the extended 30-round clips they had. He tucked them in his waistline, grabbed the Taurus Judge revolver loaded with six .410 shotgun shells. He tucked it into the ankle holster, then paused as her face popped into his mind. He had loved Yvette more than he had ever loved any other woman. She had been his heart.

He screwed up by entertaining other women, in his and Yvette's mansion's guest bedroom. She got back at him by fucking one of her employees that worked at a battered women's shelter that she and Julie had started. T.G. caught his girl in a gazebo, seconds away from putting the guy's dick in her mouth.

He underestimated the guy and got his ribs broken, then Yvette still left with the guy, leaving T.G. on the ground in excruciating pain. Then Dale and Samantha Webster showed up, sending his already destroyed life further int the deep pits of hell.

T.G. grinded his teeth. It all had him seeing red, blood boiling. He had been a good guy, somewhat, but now his soul was gone and so was his heart. He had participated in the capture of Yvette and Julie. Looking at his reflection in the mirror behind his dresser, the blood-stained bandage over his cheek was a painful reminder of what he had done to Yvette. He had no choice, though. Whatever agency Samantha was with, she could have him in a place ten times worse the USP Terre Haute.

He wasn't having that. The list of jobs that Samantha had given him, T.G. had absolutely no intention of not attempting every single one. He'd rather be pushing flowers than to be in the joint sharing showers.

Leaving out, T.G. slowed his rapidly beating heart, and focused his mind on the task at hand. He wanted to stay a free man. For that to happen, people had to die.

Chapter 2

Bucks pulled up next to the blacked-out Ford Expedition and parked. The darkness of the lot in the front of an auto salvage yard provided him and the man he was about to meet with the perfect cover. Although, he wasn't worried about anyone stumbling upon him or the lieutenant of the Illinois State Police Department.

He saw the older bald dark-skinned man standing a few feet away from the back of the government-issued SUV. Bucks killed the monster under his hood and hopped out. Even in the dark, Bucks could see the look on Lieutenant Jarvis Michaels' face.

"Talk to me," Bucks nearly pleaded, desperate to know what he would bet his life the fifty-six-year-old police veteran knew. Michaels took a deep breath, then exhaled. He took out his iPhone, went to a video clip that had been sent to him and hit play. He handed the phone to Bucks and gripped the sides of his bullet-proof vest, dreading the six-foot-two-inch tall, light brown skinned man's reaction.

Bucks watched the clip with an already heavy heart pounding in his chest. He could tell the camera was fixed on the side of a building. He could make out the highway further back from a drive-space behind the building. A few vehicles went back and forth. He then realized it was the gas station right off Tauby Avenue and I-94, ten minutes north of Chicago.

Suddenly he saw the deep blue two-door Rolls-Royce Dawn that he bought for his fiancée speed in and head right

CHRISTOPHER "DIESEL" HORNEZES

for the rear bathroom. He watched Julie skid the convertible Rolls to a stop. Yvette jumped out, holding her ass and running to the bathroom. He saw her try to open the door, but it was locked. Her face scrunched up and she waddled off the screen, likely having not made it to the toilet in time.

Bucks looked at Julie. He saw her turn around and pet both Sir and Rock's heads. They were Yvette's and Julie's K9 trained German Shepherds, fearless protectors and killers when they needed to be. Just then Bucks caught sight of a black Chevy van pulling up and parking across the way from where Julie was.

"Shit," Bucks cussed as two masked and hooded men with AK-47s hopped out. He saw Sir and Rock start barking at them. Julie turned and saw the men as they ran towards her. She panicked, reaching for what Bucks knew was a gun. The German Shepherds jumped out and attempted to attack the men, but the shooters stopped them with a barrage of bullets.

"Noo!" Bucks shouted, watching the two beloved canines be obliterated right next to Julie's car. Julie had just turned her gun in the direction of one of the shooters when he ran in and hit her arm, knocked the gun out of her hand and slammed the butt of the chopper into Julie's head, dazing her.

Michaels could see it. Bucks was at the part where the men grabbed Julie and were dragging the Vietnamese beauty towards the van kicking and screaming. Bucks' eyes filled with tears as he watched the woman he loved more than life, the woman that was carrying his baby in her belly, be thrown into the van and carted off.

Bucks almost hit "end" until he peeped Yvette staggering out towards the chaos where the dogs laid in a pool of blood, not moving. Suddenly she flew forward and hit the ground. Bucks gasped when he saw Webster step into view, wielding a shotgun. He pointed it at her face, and she rolled over, blood dripping from the back of her head. He could tell words were being exchanged. A second later, Bucks saw another van pull up. When Bucks saw who had hopped out of the van his jaw dropped.

Michaels saw it. Bucks now knew that his brother-from-another-mother had pulled the ultimate betrayal. Bucks watched T.G. grab Yvette and start to put her in the van, but not before she shot forward and bit his cheek. She bit down hard and yanked her head back. Bucks saw her rip a chunk of flesh away.

T.G. dropped her, screaming in pain as blood spewed from the gaping wound. Yvette tried to run, but Webster caught her by her hair and yanked her back. He muscled her into the van. T.G. got in behind her and closed the door, then the van sped off. For a minute, Bucks was speechless. He felt like he couldn't breathe. He halfway didn't believe what he had just seen, but there was no denying it. Julie and Yvette had been taken, and their dogs were dead.

After another minute, Bucks wiped away the tears that had rolled down his face. He felt the lieutenant lay a hand on his shoulder.

"I'm not even gonna pretend to know how you feel, son," said Michaels." But what I can say is that this is the start of a very long, and a very bloody war. One that I do not intend for us to lose. Walter has been briefed and so has our squads. This is all off the books, from this moment forward."

Bucks finally was able to take his eyes off the pothole in the ground that he had gotten lost staring at. He looked up at Michaels, with fury in his eyes.

"You got your people, I got mine," he said darkly. "But from this moment forward, ain't no talkin'...just killin'."

Without a word more, Bucks went and hopped back into his Chevy, peeling off leaving rubber track marks and smoke behind, along with Lieutenant Michaels, who felt the same rage that Bucks did.

***

"Come on! I did what you asked of me! I did that shit for months! I've had nightmares about what I was doing to her!"

He heard Samantha laughing through the speakers in his S500 Mercedes. Her laughter made him even angrier as he sat behind the wheel. Parked in a long row of vehicles at a Wal-Mart in Zion, Alfonzo had just gotten into his older car, when the devil with a badge called him. She was demanding another task of him. He was pissed. He had done so many already. He had no choice. Having gotten caught up with two dirty guns a month ago, both of them with so many bodies on them that the feds had to swoop in. Samantha showed up, with three men in suits and another woman. She refused to tell him what agency she was with, when she told him that she was not FBI, DEA, nor ATF. Whatever she was, it was powerful enough for her to make the Waukegan Police Department chief bow to her, then make his officers immediately release Alfonzo with no record of ever having arrested him.

Alfonzo was taken to a building in Sturtevant, Wisconsin, which turned out to be an abandoned storage facility. There, Samantha laid it on him. He was to woo his boss at the women's shelter he worked at. He had to make her his and then get her to open up. Samantha told him that when the time was right, he was to serve her up on a silver platter. He did so by spiking Yvette's scrambled eggs with Milk of Magnesia and a strong laxative. Samantha wanted her to be off her square when she and her husband swooped in. What better way to catch someone up when they had to take a mighty dump?

***

"You know what? You're right, Alfonzo," said Samantha. "I gave you a chance at freedom and you did what I asked. I gave you my word that if you did as I said, you would be done." Alfonzo perked up then. "So…I'm good? I don't have to do anything else?"

"No. You're done. Tah tah," Samantha replied, the call was ended.

"Yes! Yes! Yeess!" Alfonzo shouted out at the top of his lungs geeked that he didn't have to do such evil things anymore. He started his engine, put it in reverse and started looking out when a crotch-rocket skidded to a stop right behind him. Alfonzo hit the brakes and cursed at the helmeted rider.

"Come on! Move, goddammit!" he shouted, beeping his horn.

The rider kicked the Ninja's kickstand out and leaned the still idling bike on it. Alfonzo's eyebrows furrowed as the rider got off the bike.

"Oh, this guy wants to raise an issue?" Alfonzo put his car in park. He opened his door and as he went to get out, he reached under his seat with his left hand, grabbing the .380 he had stashed.

The rider walked towards him. Alfonzo shot up with the little semi-auto in his hand.

"Take another step and I'll shoot your ass, dude! Move your bike and leave, and we can forget this ever happened!" Alfonzo said, gripping his gun tightly to keep the rider from seeing how much he was trembling with fear. Alfonzo had never fired a gun in his life. The Walther PPK wasn't even loaded. He saw the rider lean to the left and crane his neck a little further, looking around him. Thinking that in some diabolical way that Samantha had popped up, Alfonzo spun around, gun up to intimidate. Nobody was there. He turned back around and found himself staring at two big cannons with extended clips.

BOC! BOC! BOC! BOC! BOC! BOC!
BOC! BOC! BOC! BOC! BOC! BOC!

***

T.G. hit him six times each with both of his Glocks. People screamed and ran for dear life. Some ducked for cover, thinking they were going to be the next victim of senseless mass shootings. Alfonzo's chest opened up. His throat and face exploded before he went down. T.G. stepped up and looked down at the dead man. His hatred for the man was amplified, for it was Alfonzo's dick that had been seconds away from being put in Yvette's mouth in a gazebo outside a popular Italian restaurant, just over a week ago. Alfonzo had also been the one that had hit him with a big tree branch and broke a couple of his ribs. Samantha made Alfonzo a target for T.G. When he got the file with Alfonzo's photo and ways to track him, he went to the very top of the list.

***

"Freeze! Police! Drop your weapon now!"

T.G. heard the cop behind him.

"Drop it!"

T.G. dropped one of his guns, knowing the one in his right hand had not been seen.

"On your knees! Now!"

Sinking down, T.G. went down to his knees. The second he heard the cop radioing for back up, he spun with the quickness and fired, hitting the cop right in his nose. The undercover officer that hid out in the store to prevent thefts flew backwards and hit the ground. Blood poured out of the big hole in the back of his head.

T.G. grabbed his other gun, ran and hopped back on the crotch-rocket. He sped out of the parking lot, leaving two bodies and crowds of terrified shoppers. *On to the next one*, he thought, as he blew down Route 173, heading towards Sheridan Road.

***

BOOM!

Bucks squeezed the trigger on the sawed-off shotgun and blew the door to T.G.'s hideaway to pieces. He ran inside, barrel up and ready to blow again. Behind him four men, no mask were equipped with fully automatic AA-12s, with 25-round drums loaded with deer-shot shells. Bucks ran towards the stairway that led to the bedrooms. Behind him, the green-eyed Dominican that had long cornrows in his head, wearing all black, had his automatic 12-gauge clutched tightly in his grasp. The other three Dominicans, all of them kin to the cocaine drug lord, went separate ways, desperately hoping that the girls were there. Bucks hit every room, while Javier Valdez watched his back. The searches came up fruitless.

"Fuck!" cursed Bucks.

He led Javi back down to the first floor, just as Javi's younger, but bigger brother Xavier awaited, with a forlorn look etched in his face. He shook his head, signifying that he had no luck either. Javi and Xavier's two older massive body-builder size cousins, Macho and Tool, both of them with long dreadlocks, came up from checking the basement.

"Not here, yo," the Dominican-Puerto Rican mixed billionaire Steel City Mafia boss Tool told Bucks.

Bucks cursed. "On everything I love, Joe. If one hair on my lady's head, or Yvette's is harmed, everybody responsible is gon' die so muthafuckin painfully!"

"Nigga, even if they came up outta this lookin' like the beautiful goddesses that they are, we still finna splatter every bitch ass nigga involved," said Javi, who had grown a very strong bond with Bucks, the ladies, and before his betrayal, T.G.

"And on my raise's grave," said Macho, the Pittsburgh, PA native speaking upon his deceased mother the way they did in the hood he and his older brother were from. "When we find dude, please do not hesitate to utilize the various methods of completely disappearin' a muthafucka that we have."

Bucks nodded.

Xavier, the strong silent type, said not a word. There was nothing to say. There were two women somewhere that they didn't want to be, and one was pregnant with Bucks' child. Bucks grabbed his phone from the pocket of his jeans. "I'm puttin' word out on the streets, two hundred fifty thousand on T.G.'s head," he said to the Valdez quad, as he began typing a text he was going to group send to his goons.

"I got half a mil on that," Macho said.

"Me too," Tool added.

"So do I," Xavier threw in finally speaking.

"I got a whole millie on it," Javi then said, bringing the bounty on T.G.'s head to two point five million. "Put the word out to everyone you know will hunt dude the fuck down. My wife and ChaCha will continue usin' their sources to locate him."

"My wife and my woman are on it too," Macho added.

Bucks sighed, beyond scared for Julie and Yvette. There was no inkling at all, where they had been taken, if they were still there, or they were even alive still.

***

"Why do you people feel it's okay to off cops like they are just bugs?"

T.G. smirked at the text he had received from Samantha. He typed a reply. "He was," T.G. told her, then sent it.

Posted up next to his bike, T.G. waited for the time to hit midnight. Studying his next target's moves for the last week, it was time to make his move. Tonight, it will be her last.

"Cops are here to PROTECT people! Not to be killed by drug-dealers! DO NOT DO IT AGAIN!" came Samantha's reply.

"Shut up, bitch," T.G. verbalized to himself, then he tucked his phone and waited in the darkness, for his time to strike.

Chapter 3

Bucks arrived at B&T Auto Imports, a big exotic and foreign automobile dealership in the Lake Forest area of Lake County, that he had gone half on with T.G. Just seeing the sign made him see red. He had known T.G. virtually his whole life. The treacherous betrayal hurt him more than he was comfortable with admitting. It brought tears to his eyes as he pulled up to where the big and tall service section garage door was. He took a deep breath, calming his nerves. He knew that now was not the time to let his emotions get out of check. He had a mission to accomplish and whether it was to find his woman and Yvette alive or to handle the traitors in their honor, Bucks was not letting none of the deceitful people that were responsible live.

***

He rolled into the big service area once the door rose up. Inside were a few very expensive exotic vehicles, and a few ol schools that even Jay Leno would pine after. Bucks closed the garage back and parked his SS next to where his silver Ferrari SF90 Stradale was. Killing the engine, he hopped out and went to his office.

In his lush foreign race car-theme office, Bucks used a non-traceable phone to place a few calls. He had met a few people along the way to the top, besides the Valdez family. For Julie, he would pay the entire world to help him get her and Yvette back. His own iPhone dinged from a text message as he finished his last call. He saw it was from Flip.

"Lots of eyes are open now," was all he said. Bucks sent a nodding emoji as a reply. Getting back up, he grabbed the key fob to the Vitesse edition Bugatti Veyron that had been delivered to him, fully loaded by Javi's younger sister. He left out of the office, re-entered the garage and hopped into the multi-million-dollar gray and black roadster, firing up the ridiculously powerful, quad turbo 16-cylinder engine. He opened the garage and pulled out with a care package up in the trunk where the engine would normally be.

***

Denise entered the small mom n' pop diner, ready to start her shift. It was her third night back, after her maternity leave time had run out. With a new baby at home, she needed to make as much money as she could to support herself and her daughter. Her baby daddy was out of the picture, sitting in a cell in the feds. Trafficking humans got him football numbers without football pay. Now she was on her own. The things that she did have, most of them came from selling the few valuable assets that he had left behind that the feds couldn't prove were purchased by illegally acquired money.

For her and her daughter's survival, Denise would do anything. From working a punk ass job for mediocre tips, to stashing a large quantity of drugs on a dirty cop in order to get out of possible federal charges that had been threatened to fall upon her, because of her baby daddy. Denise was a survivor. If you were not her or her daughter, you were food, and they had to eat to stay alive.

***

Sighing to herself, she walked through the semi-crowded restaurant to get to the rear employee section to clock in.

Though it was the graveyard shift, Denise was still astounded that so many people came to eat at a 50s-era-style diner. The people of Winthrop Harbor, a small town in between Zion and Pleasant Prairie, Wisconsin, were mostly white and allegedly had a strong KKK presence there. A few of the normal patrons were undoubtedly a part of the racist organization.

Denise, a beautiful woman with luscious curves, skin that was the color of cocoa, with long dreadlocks dyed blondish brown, was often hit on and ogled by so many of them. There weren't many men, racist or not, that could deny a gorgeous black woman.

***

"Hey Denise. Busy night tonight," said the older white woman, frying up some sausage in an old cast iron skillet, dressed in the same bright pink waitress dress that Denise was wearing.

"Yeah. Hope that means a bunch of tips, Bertha," Denise replied, clocking in at the machine opposite the main stove.

Cherry, a young white girl with blonde hair and blue eyes, was in the baker's section rolling out dough to make her famous cherry pie. Adam, the main cook, was frying and grilling, sweating his ass off from working so hard. Then there was Hollie, the cold-food prep girl that tried to create salads and fruit dishes with bright vibrant colors. She was what people called a "free spirit."

"Come on hun." Bertha chuckled. "Out of all of us, you are the one that takes home the most tips. You're young n' very beautiful. These ol' geezers come here to eat pie 'n see you."

Denise smiled. Feeling liked and desired was something that she only felt at work. It made her feel like she was alive still.

"You go on n' get to work now," Bertha said, dumping the crispy sausage patties on a plate with toasted bread, "and make sure I see that little one of yours soon."

"I will," Denise assured her, then after she grabbed a clean apron and put it on, washed her hands, she made her way out to the floor to go take some orders.

***

"Hello, sir. What can I get for you tonight?" Denise said, with her note pad and pen.

"Lemme get one of those sausage things that's like a pancake burger, please? And some scrambled eggs."

Denise wrote the order down.

"And to drink, sir?"

"Apple juice, please."

"Wow. Two pleases? I normally never get one," Denise said, then for the first time since stopping at the window booth table he sat in that was in her section, she looked at the guy.

Oh my...this nigga is handsome as fuck. He has to either be married, has ten kids, or is a jailbird. Nope! But still, for a minute as he smiled, she felt it very hard to turn away. He was light brown skinned, rocking Fendi and diamond jewelry. His bald fade was fresh, waves up top lining so sharply done that it would make Steve Harvey wish he had his hair still. She could tell he had some muscle, and he was tall. He was just her type, but Denise had taken her mind off of men, due to the crap with her baby daddy.

"Nobody says please to you? That ain't cool," the guy said to her. "I grew up hearin' that please and thank you are the magic words."

"Hey, Mister! Mister!"

An older man rushed up to the table just then. His face was lit up as if he was in front of a celebrity.

"Is that your car outside? That gray and black one?" Denise subconsciously looked outside the window. She could see what looked like a spaceship parked outside the window. A couple of people were standing in front of it, gawking at it as if it was something they would never see pass through their hick-ass town again.

"Yes, it's mine," Denise heard the guy say. She turned and looked at him, surprised that a man dressed like that was pushing such an exotic ride, was in a lame ass diner, instead of at a Ruth Kris or Benihana's.

"Oh, man! It's a Ferrari, right?" the old man asked.

"No, sir. It's a Bugatti."

"Hot dog! I met a guy that had a Bugatti! Wooo!"

The old guy left. Denise chuckled as he exited the diner.

"You have a nice laugh."

She looked at the man. He was looking up at her.

"Um…thank you…uh?"

"They call me Bucks. What's your name?"

"I'm…Denise. It's nice to meet you. Um…I'll go put your order in…Bucks."

She hurried off, feeling clowned out for stammering. He had to have thought she was a goofy bitch.

***

Denise delivered him his order, then went to tend to her other patrons. A half hour later, she noticed Bucks get up, finished with his meal. She had been right. He was definitely tall. He dwarfed her, as she was only five three and a half inches tall. She saw him look up right at her. He pulled a wad of cash out of his pocket. Thinking he was likely a good tipper, Denise anticipated him leaving her a twenty. He peeled off a new hundred-dollar-bill and dropped it on the table. Nodding his head, he took his leave, exiting the diner and hopping into the expensive car.

Denise and everyone inside hear the powerful engine start. It rolled out of the parking spot, merged onto Sheridan Road and shot off like a speeding bullet heading north.

"Wow." Denise was astonished as she picked up the C-note.

"That nigga is a straight heartbreaker, I bet."

***

For the rest of her shift, Denise worked hard and collected tips. By six in the morning, she made herself just over two hundred dollars in tips. Happy with that, she clocked out, bid the others adieu and made her way out to where her ages-old Nissan Sentra was parked to the side of the lot, away from the other vehicles. She hit the unlock button and got inside. She put her key inside the ignition, started the engine then screamed when she saw a man with a hood pulled up on his head in the backseat.

"Shhhhhh!" He raised the gun up so she could see he meant business. "No more screamin', shortie, or I'ma have to silence you."

"Wh-what d-do you want? Please don't hurt me! I have a newborn at home!"

He chuckled. "You think that means anything to a nigga wit a thumper in the back of yo' car, waitin' for you? You pissed Samantha off!"

Denise gasped when she heard the name. She swore that she had gotten free of the work, after doing all that shit for her, to keep her freedom and her daughter. She started crying. There was no way she was making it home to her baby. Samantha did not fuck around.

"It's all good, lil mama," she heard the guy tell her. "It'll be quick and painless. Close your eyes and count down from three."

Denise said a prayer, asking the Lord to take care of her little girl and to forgive her for her sins.

"Okay, lil mama. Time's up. Three…two…one…"

***

Trunk empty of the thirty bricks of raw Dominican cocaine, big leather Gucci bags full of cash from the hand off, Bucks headed back south down Sheridan, closing in on Winthrop Harbor. He was glad to be out of Racine. He hated Racine, Kenosha, Pleasant Prairie. Wisconsin was not for a black man.

"What the hell?" Bucks saw a large number of fire trucks and police vehicles with their lights flashing up ahead. He realized they were in front of the diner where he had just been. Slowing down as he got closer, a crotch-rocket zipped past him so fast in the opposite direction that it was like a blur.

The vehicles in front of him were going turtle as they got to the front where the diner's turn in was. Bucks looked to his left and with the tall parking lot lights on, he was able to catch a glimpse of a smoldering car, that was parked off to the side of the lot.

"Oh snap," he said, seeing a burning body being pulled out of the car. "Whoever that was they must have pissed someone off."

The traffic started rolling again. Bucks went around them and used half of the staggering amount of horsepower to get home. He was dead-tired and needed to recharge his batteries for what was to come next.

***

T.G. stepped lightly, clutching his cannon in his hand. He moved about as quietly as he could throughout his spot. It was a mess. Someone had been there. He looked in every room, the bathroom, closets, the attic, then the basement. After twenty long minutes, T.G. was sure that whoever had kicked his door in was gone…for now. Going back to the door, T.G. stepped out to the hallway. He looked at her. She looked terrified.

"We can't stay here," he told her, taking his gun.

Denise looked at him. Her eyes were filled with tears and were puffy.

"Why? You were sent to kill me, but you didn't," she said.

An hour ago, she had been prepared to die. T.G. had other plans. He had told her that he could never murder a woman with an infant child. His plan was simple, fake her death. Gruesomely, he murdered a young guy that had come out of the restaurant with a build similar to Denise's, put his corpse in the car, and burned it. He knew with all the technology these days it was very possible for crime scene and forensic technicians to find out that it was not Denise in the car. But knowing Samantha, one look at the news feeds on social media, "Young waitress dies in car fire outside of her job at diner," T.G. knew her focus would shift to the next target she had T.G. on.

"I have a bad past," T.G. told her, feeling so ashamed of what he did to Yvette. "The way life is for me now, I want to be as righteous as I can be, before I meet death." Denise nodded in understanding. She knew that whatever was on his heart, it was very heavy. *He can't be that bad…he saved my life*, she thought.

"I have a car stashed around back. I want you to stick with me, because when Samantha finds out you're alive, she not gon' be just at you."

The thought of Samantha's wrath sent chills up Denise's spine.

"I need to get my daughter."

T.G. nodded. He took the keys to his 88' Chevy IROC-Z Camaro out of his pocket. He gave them to her.

"You drive. I'll shout if any dummies come too close." Denise followed T.G. back out of the building, exiting through the rear and coming to where his clean black IROC sat and gleaming chrome IROC rims.

They hopped in. Denise started the engine, put it in drive and pulled off, praying again to the Man above, that whatever was to happen to her, that he protect her little girl and give her a good life.

Chapter 4

Bucks woke up feeling like he had not gotten a wink of sleep. Everything felt and looked surreal, like he was stuck in one big bad dream. Waking up to an empty bed hurt his heart. No matter what business was being handled, he and his woman had always made it home to each other.

For a while, he lay there. His mind was already racing. "Where was she? How the hell did Webster get the drop on her and Yvette? Where did T.G. fit into all of this?" Bucks needed answers. He needed them now.

***

He got up, hit his grille and swished his mouthwash. After a long hot shower, he got dressed in a Versace fit with the leather and alligator Versace jacket. The black ceramic Cartier Asometrice timepiece tied in with his black swag. One long yellow-gold Cuban link chain went around his neck, diamond studs went in both ears, and he put on all-black Virgil Abloh Nike Air Force One low-tops. He rubbed on some cologne then took a second to scroll through his iPhone. As he looked through his contact, he got a text from Lieutenant Michaels.

"Turn on Channel 7 ABC News."

Bucks turned the Chicagoland news on and saw a segment on Julie and Yvette's abduction.

"Early yesterday evening, two female sergeants with Illinois State Police were abducted from a gas station near

Rosemont. It was a brutal scene, so violent that we cannot show you the video. Moments prior to the abduction, two K9s were shot to death when they hopped out of Sergeant Julie Tran's car to attack the men in masks. They were able to overpower her and threw her in a van. Sergeant Yvette Jones had gone inside to use the restroom. She was seen minutes later, hopping into a vehicle out in the front and leaving the scene."

"What the fuck?" Bucks rewound the segment with his remote, thinking he was tripping.

He heard it again. The media was saying Yvette had set Julie up to be taken.

Bucks immediately called Michaels.

"I know. Believe me, I know, son," the ol' head answered.

"How in the actual fuck is that possible? Yvette would never get down on Julie! They're like sisters!"

"We both know what we saw on the video I had, Bucks."

"Excuse me! You said, 'had'?"

Bucks heard Michaels groan with frustration.

"My phone has been wiped. Somehow, I was hacked. The video is gone, and nobody at the department can recover it."

Bucks was floored by what he was hearing. Life had just gotten crazier.

"Look. For now, lay low, we have no clue who has this type of influence to manipulate the damn media, but whoever it is, they are likely someone that is very bad," Michaels said. "And you're not gonna like this, but this is me being a thirty-year veteran on the force. This individual is going through great lengths to hide Dale Webster's involvement and paint Yvette as the guilty one. This tells me that they have plans for Yvette and Julie, which likely means they are not dead."

Bucks sighed in relief. He knew there was more to come though.

"This also means they are both in serious danger, and for the time being…they are on their own."

He started grinding his teeth. He was so pissed, so filled with anger, that he broke down in tears. He was unable to hold it in any longer.

"Why is this happenin', man?" Bucks managed to ask as tears fell. "They ain't even do R. Kelly's weird ass this bad, Joe!"

"Son, when I find out, you find out, and we will handle it," Michaels stated.

"I vow to not let this stand, Bernard, but this is a grave situation. We cannot move wrong, son. Do you understand?"

"Yeah. Just tell me where and when to be whenever, and I'm there. On my baby, Lieutenant."

"You've got my word. Keep me posted too, if you hear anything."

The call ended then. Bucks took in a deep breath, then exhaled. He repeated this three times and felt no better. *Shit was so fucked up. All for what? Who in God's name could manipulate the media?*

Bucks couldn't think of a single answer to any of the questions in his head. And it was making him even angrier.

***

"Good job," Samantha said, to the broadcast network boss, giving him a sly smile. "You will be compensated for your hard work, Mr. Bundy. The tall old white man shook his head. "I took an oath to give Chicagoans the truth about daily events in our city. You just made me break it. How am I supposed to live with myself?"

"Well, with a big bag of money destined to be delivered to you, I'd manage quite comfortably. Besides…the girl your reporters painted to be the one who orchestrated all this, she's just a peon cop. Don't feel bad." The man felt horrible. Samantha could see it in his eyes. He was soft.

"When do I get my money?" Mr. Bundy asked her.

"My associate will bring it to our home. Make plans for a long vacation in paradise, my good man," Samantha said, smiling at him, then turning on her five-inch heels and sauntering off, swinging her hips enticingly as she headed for the chauffeured SUV awaiting her out front of the skyscraper the news studio was in.

***

The armed agent standing posted at the rear passenger-side door opened it and took her hand to help her into the luxurious Escalade. She got seated in the reclining captain's chair and took the iPad sitting on the seat next to her. As the driver pulled off, Samantha sent an encrypted message to her asset, then pressed the button at her right. The forty-eight-inch HDTV that was also a partition rolled down. The man in the passenger's seat turned back and looked at her, momentarily distracted by the view of her pink panties from under her skirt.

"Uh...yes, ma'am?" he asked, averting his eyes up to hers. Samantha smirked at him. Playing with the guy, she nonchalantly opened her legs a little wider.

"I'm hungry," she said, and licked her lips.

"Okay. Where...would you like to...go?" he asked, trying so hard not to look up her skirt again.

"Hmmm. How about you decide, Bentz. What are you hungry for?" Samantha said, then she opened her legs even wider. Bentz's jaw started moving like one of those plastic chattering teeth toys, dick hardening in his trousers.

"Pie," he told her, as the driver came to a red light and stopped. "Sweet pie."

Samantha then closed and overlapped her right leg over her left.

"Well, act like it then," she said, then hit the button and put the partition back up, with a smile on her face, and wet ass pussy.

***

Flip entered the big 12-car garage and went to where Bucks was standing next to his woman's dark blue Bentley Flying Spur. He embraced Bucks like a brother. He knew his mans was fucked up behind all the shit. Flip wanted to be there for his homie, like a real friend was.

I know I said it before, but I'ma say it again. A nigga here for you, bruh," Flip said to Bucks. "You ain't' alone in this. JuJu and Yvette good people, to be cops n' shid. I'ma ride wit' cha' til the wheels fall off and we pushin' Beemer, Benzes and Bentley, the wheels on them muhfuckas don't fall off ever."

Bucks nodded his head, appreciative of Flip's words.

"What's the word? Anybody seen him?" Bucks asked.

"Naw. His car's gone from his spot and a bike's there, but nobody saw him come or go. Javi nor his people have tracked him yet."

Bucks shook his head. "He and I think the same, Flip. We know how to hide in plain sight when people are lookin' for us. I would bet everything I am that T.G. is close…very close, because he has investments in the streets too and even with two-and-a-half million on his head, I guarantee that he has people out there that will turn on him."

"I agree, I remember how he got his name. He a truly grimy nigga and goon. A lot of people fear a nigga that's real."

"Well, be that as it may, T.G. violated the code and he has to feel it. He gotta pay, bro, Period." Nodding his head in agreement, Flip dapped Bucks up again.

"So, I hear we been havin' a little competition out in Zompton?" Bucks asked them.

"Them wannabes in those apartment on 27th and Galilee tryna' move shit and step on me?"

"Yep. We been lettin' em' have their fun. This situation wit' the lil mommas have been what we all been focused on."

"I was told to hold up on them, a good source relayed to me that whoever's doin this isn't the type to just off 'em. They are alive, but they aren't safe."

Flip thought about it. Having heard how the two beautiful lady cops got down, it very much sounded like they were Pit Bull-tested tough. The only thing was, Julie was pregnant. A pregnant woman could only do but so much when it a dire situation.

"This what we gon' do, bro," Flip said, and stopped close to his homie. "We gon' ask Big Homie up in the clouds for help. He will deliver, not just JuJu and Yvette back to our family, but he gon' deliver the bitches that did them like that. This gon' be the one time where He allows vengeance to be ours, you dig I'm sayin', my nigga?"

Bucks nodded his head.

"Good. Bow yo' head and let's holla. Dear Heavenly Father, my bro and I stand here askin' you, to help us bring JuJu and Yvette back to us safe and sound, along with my man's child. We also ask you to allow us to holla at the clowns that broke up our family. And last, Father God, we plead with you that you stop lettin' bitchass niggas and snake ass hoes be born. Real niggas and real women only. Say it wit' me, Bucks."

"Amen!" they said in unison.

"Cool. Now let's go do some gangsta shit," Flip said pulling his iPhone out and hitting GB and Law via text.

***

"Aaah!" screamed Denise, jumping out of her sleep. Her loud scream woke her two-month-old daughter. She started crying, terrified of the sudden sound.

"Oh noo! I'm very sorry, Letoya!" Denise scooped her baby up and cradled her. "Shhhh. It's okay, baby. Mama's sorry."

Letoya slowly started calming down. Denise rocked back and forth, humming a sweet melody. As she did, she looked around the bedroom she was in. It was like a suite in a five-star hotel. She barely remembered going to the condominium. She did remember driving with T.G. to go pick her baby up. Her home girl, who babysat the little one, was worried like never before when Denise frantically rushed to pack up as much of her and Letoya's clothes as she could. Then T.G. came in and spooked the piss out of her friend.

On the way from Denise's apartment in downtown Waukegan, out to Fox Lake, far from anyone that knew T.G., she had been so tired that T.G. had to take the wheel. When they got to the quaint home in the quiet recesses of the suburbs, Denise was damn near dead on her feet. T.G. carried their things in, helped get them situated with food and whatever to drink, a tour of the house and a tutorial on the security system. He left them to settle in and went to regroup in his room.

***

A knock at the door came. Denise scooted off the bed and went to answer the door. T.G. was outside of it. He was naked, save for the towel wrapped around his waist. Denise instantly froze when she saw how sculpted and tattooed he was.

Holy shit! He is…holy shit! She thought, eyeing him hard.

"Hey! I heard a scream, then lil mama cryin'. Everything alright?" T.G. asked her.

Denise hadn't heard a word that he had said. Her eyes were stuck on his ripped physique.

"Denise? Hey?"

Finally, she looked up at him. "Huh?"

"I was checkin' on you. I heard a scream, then Letoya cryin'.""

"Oh...yeah...it was just a bad dream. We're okay, T.G. Thank you for checkin' on us."

"Tremaine!"

Denise heard a woman's voice, then she saw the Hispanic chick walk up to T.G.'s side, wearing a towel around her upper body.

"What's taking so long, papi?" she whined.

Denise's eyebrows furrowed. For some odd reason, she grew extremely jealous. Seeing the girl all up on T.G. made Denise want to put her daughter down and beat the bitch up.

"I swear, I told you to wait in the room, Brandi! Take ya ass back and sit down, Joe!"

Brandi smacked her lips at him. Looking at Denise, she curled her lip up, then stomped off angrily.

"Sorry about that, Denise."

She looked at him. "It's...fine."

"You hungry? I'ma make breakfast."

Denise was indeed hungry, but she wasn't in a rush to see T.G.'s honey dip anytime soon.

"I know you're hungry, so don't even cap. You ain't' ate nothin' since the previous night, and you got a baby to feed, which means you gotta feed you," T.G. said. "So, go shower, get lil mama together and meet me in the kitchen."

"I don't need ya girlfriend getting crazy with me, T.G. I'm not for that gum-bumpin' that these bum-ass bitches do."

T.G. laughed. "I give you my word, Denise, by the time you get done feedin' Letoya, shorty will be already in an Uber, cussin' me out for kickin' her out."

He left then to handle that, leaving a smile growing on Denise's face. She looked down at her baby. Letoya was yawning, ready to go back to sleep.

"Uh, oh! Somebody's still 'sheepie'!" Denise nuzzled her daughter's nose, getting a giggle out of her. "Let's get some milk in that tummy first, then you can go back to sleep, while I end up havin' to whoop a bitch around T.G."

Chapter 5

"Maaan, this nigga dun' lost his muthafuckin' mind," Hood snapped, as he and his homies looked out of the shattered window of their dope spot's living room. They had been bagging up heroin, laced with fentanyl and crack, gearing up to flood their little apartment complex in Zion. They had that shit, and the fiends that lived in the six tall and wide buildings on the corner of 27th and Galilee flew to them like angels warding off demons. Friends from all around Zompton, or the Zag as many called Zion now, flocked to them. Hood and a few of his guys had burned down other trap houses belonging to the competition, destroying hundreds of thousands of dollars in order to make the cluckers come to them.

A brick came flying through the window, startling all six of them. They hurried to grab their Dracos and ARPs, ready to fan down whoever had done such a foolish thing.

***

Hood saw the crackhead standing there on the center walkway that ran between the buildings. He was dirty, hair and beard looking rough. He just stood there, as if he had not just done the unthinkable.

"Yo' ass dead, Jack!" Hood shouted out the broken window.

Jack pulled out a glass pipe, a lighter that he had turned into a torch, and he started piping up right there. Hood and his guys all watched the man take a big hit, then blow out a thick cloud of smoke.

"That's funny 'cause I don't feel dead! I feel good! Wooo!" Jack shouted and raised his pipe back to his lips.

"Aye, Will, go snake that nigga up and make him move around, Joe!" Hood ordered, seeing no point in blowing a cluck down and getting his zone hot.

Will, a muscular high-yellow dude of average height, rocking a black tee, jeans, and Air Forces, made his way to the door to get at the fiend, while Red, Kenny, Local, and Bread posted with Hood. Will unlocked all four locks and opened the door. The second he did, a fist with brass knuckles came flying into his jaw, instantly breaking it.

"Shit!" Hood cussed as two large, blue-nosed Pit Bulls ran into the apartment, right to Bread and Local. They didn't even get the chance to shoot before the dogs jumped on them, chomping down on their arms, and biting down hard. Kenny and Red took aim at them as Local and Bread screamed in pain.

BRRRRRRR! BRRRRRRR!

BRRRRRRR! BRRRRRRR!

Hood found himself covered in blood and brains from both Kenny and Red when the man that had seemingly appeared out of thin air blew twin MAC 11s into the apartment, doming Kenny and Red before they could shoot the dogs. Hood grew irate. He painted his Draco at the hooded shooter and got ready to put him down, when he heard a whistle come from behind him. He spun around to pop whoever it was.

SMACK! SMACK!

"Aahh! What the fuuck!" Hood shouted, as two raw eggs splattered in his face. He jumped back, trying to get the egg out of his eyes, still hearing Local and Bully screaming in pain while the dogs ripped them up.

Hood cleared his vision just a little. Enough to see a dark figure in a hoodie with a SpongeBob SquarePants mask on walking towards him. He backtracked, getting close to the window. A pair of hands grabbed him from behind and yanked him out of the window, slamming him to the ground. Hood yelped in pain when his head smacked the concrete hard. The sounds of sirens wailing out from close by made him feel relieved that the cops were coming. The Zion police station was literally three minutes away.

"Aye, Hood?"

He looked up and saw the figure with the SpongeBob mask on standing over him.

"All that sound means is that yo' bitch ass guys bodies gon' get scraped up," the man said. "But you, my nigga, are comin' with me." A blunt object then come down hard on Hood's face, knocking him clean out.

***

Bucks told Flip, G.B. and Law to take Hood to the whip. Flip called to his dogs Rex and Zo, then Hood was carried off.

"Aye, big man, you still got me?"

Bucks looked at Jack, as lights from cop cars racing up Galilee lit the area up.

"Yup. I gotcha."

In a flash, Bucks upped his Glock 19 and knocked the crackhead's shit back. He would never trust a cluck to hold strong with incriminating evidence, when the cops came for him.

***

Dipping through the building's pathway, past apartments with residents looking out of their windows, Bucks ran to the stolen Durango where Law sat behind the wheel, parked in a dark cut on the east side of the complex. Law calmly exited the area as cops flew into it on the west side, busting a left onto 27th and made a clean getaway, with the unconscious fool held captive by Bucks' goons.

***

He cursed, angry that Samantha was ignoring his calls, texts, and his emails. Beyond pissed, Mr. Bundy yanked the steering wheel of his restored 1968 Chevy Chevelle SS to the left and entered the driveway to his lavish home out in Evanston. Rolling up the brick-paved road, he arrived at his house and parked at the front door. His wife Hilda opened the French front doors and hurried out, wearing a silk robe and a frown on her face.

"What's wrong?" Mr. Bundy asked his wife, as she ran into his arms.

"There's a man here! He has a bag full of money, honey!"

"Oh." Mr. Bundy chuckled. "It's okay, hun, he's here to pay me for a bet that I won. Let's go inside and get ready to go on a long vacation," he told her, reaching around and palming her perky ass.

***

Inside their home, Mr. Bundy led his wife to the dining room, where she said the man was. Sitting in a chair at the smoked glass dinner table, Mr. Bundy saw the dark-brown skinned man there. He had on a dark blue hoodie, jeans, and Jordans. A leather duffel bag sat on the table. The zipper was open. Mr. Bundy could see the cash inside of it. The guy stood to his full six-foot-tall height, towering over the broadcast network boss, and his wife.

"Samantha thanks you for your cooperation," he said with a smirk.

Without another word, he walked around them and took his leave.

"Harvey? The guy said cooperation, you said a 'bet.' What is going on?" Hilda asked, as her husband went and picked the bag up by its handles.

"What's going on is you and I, baby cakes, are going on a long and beautiful vacation, thanks to this." He went to lift the bag and winced when he felt a jolt of pain strike his shoulder. "Wowzer, this thing is heavy. Must be a lot of little bills in here."

"Harvey, I don't like this. Something doesn't feel right," said Hilda as she watched him start pulling out banded stacks of tens, twenties and fifties.

"Oh, it will, honey. Especially when we're makin' love out on a terrace at a luxurious hotel in Paris." Mr. Bundy then frowned when he saw a little cardboard box inside. "What is this?" He pulled it out and discovered that it was what made the bag so heavy.

"What is that?" Hilda asked.

"Only one way to find out, babe," said Mr. Bundy, then went to get a knife to cut through the thick tape wrapped all around it.

***

"Everything okay? Denise asked when T.G. got back in the car and quickly started the engine.

"Yup." He put it in drive and hurried off. Grabbing his phone from the center console, he called Samantha. She answered immediately. "The customer was very happy with their package," T.G. said, then ended the call. Denise's eyebrows furrowed, wondering how the goon had gone from hitter to delivery boy.

BOOM!

The explosion shook Denise. A fireball rose up into the sky, lighting it up. As she whipped her head around and looked back out of the rear window, seeing that the fireball had come from the house T.G. had gone to, Letoya started crying. The blast woke her up, scaring the hell out of her. Denise hurried to unstrap her and pulled her out of the baby seat. She cradled Letoya in her arms, holding her tight, singing a soft lullaby to her to calm her down. T.G. couldn't help but smile with admiration. He was very fond of women who were good mothers, but even more so when it came to good Black mothers. He wished that Letoya's father was around, but life was not fair.

At that moment, T.G. made a silent vow to himself. He swore to be the person Denise and Letoya needed in their lives, whether as a friend, or a financial source. He craved salvation of his soul for what he did to Yvette and Julie. The more T.G. thought about it, the more he loathed himself. He could only imagine what Bucks must be on, whenever they crossed paths.

"What does she have on you?" Denise asked just then, which brought T.G. out of his thoughts.

"What did you say?" Cruising along a dark two-way road, he glanced over at Denise to see her eyes on him.

"That woman has somethin' on you that's makin' you handle her dirty work. What is it?"

T.G. chuckled. "More than most so-called gangstas can say they did, let alone lie about. Believe, me though, I know what I'm doin.'"

Denise continued staring at him for another minute. She couldn't understand why, but she felt safe. She felt like both she and her daughter were in good hands. And she had no plans on leaving those hands, until she found some sort of way to put Samantha down.

The bitch was going to have to go. Denise was ready to use T.G. to get to her and hoped to God that it wouldn't backfire on her, her daughter, or him.

"What happened to your face?" she asked him then. She'd wanted to know, since she first saw the bloody gauze bandage on his cheek.

T.G. sighed. "Karma is what happened, shortie."

Denise had a clue what he meant but decided that at the moment it didn't matter. She looked down and saw Letoya was knocked out again. She smiled at her darling little angel and kissed Letoya's head. For the rest of the ride back to T.G.'s house, the only sounds came from Megan Thee Stallion, Tee Grizzley, Kendrick Lamar, Doja Cat, and the V8 engine under the IROC's hood.

***

"Aaaaaaaaagggghhhh! Fuuuuuuck!" Hood screamed in agony when Bucks blew crushed shards of glass into his eyes. Hanging upside down, bound by his ankles by a thick rope and hoisted up over a fenced baseball field's home plate, Hood was going nowhere fast.

Bucks, Flip, G.B., and Law stood around him, all of them with Louisville Sluggers in their grasp. They had taken him to Zion-Benton High School to handle the competition. There was no mercy in store for Hood.

CRACK!

Flip swung his bat and hit Hood in his right side, breaking his ribs. Hood screamed out at the tops of his lungs. G.B. swung his bat and broke Hood's left ribs. Law swung and obliterated Hood's tailbone. Bucks took Hood's kneecaps out. Broken up and in so much pain, Hood's bladder and his bowels released. His urine leaked down and soaked his face.

He heard footsteps get close to him, then he heard Buck's voice.

"Aye, Hood? Bet you wish you would've left the Zoo when it closed, huh? When the real gorillas came to replace you and yo punk bitch orangutans." Hood shook and trembled. He hurt all over. He couldn't see a thing because his eyeballs were sliced and cut up from the tiny shards in between them and his eyelids.

"Don't trip, though, homie. Maybe wherever you are about to go will be better for you, but out here, I am the man," he heard Bucks say.

Hood then heard Flip shout, "Get him!" He cried for help out loud, then felt two sets of sharp teeth sink into his face and his neck. He thrashed and begged as the dogs ripped and yanked. One of the dogs clamped his jaws over Hood's face. He chomped down so hard that Hood literally felt his face breaking.

Bucks and his guys watched Rex and Zo rip Hood apart. Rex ate Hood's face. Zo snatched his Adam's apple out and devoured it. Flip called to them when the lifeless body leaked blood down on home plate. They obeyed and went to their human with bloody muzzles and wagging tails. Flip praised them for a job well done, exciting them even more.

"Take the body to the landfill and bury it," Bucks told his guys.

"Why not just let him stay? As a warning to any other clowns that think they get wild like us?" G.B. asked.

Bucks looked at his guys. "Do you wanna be responsible for givin' a high school kid nightmares when they see a dead, ate-up body hangin' from a baseball diamond fence?"

"Nope." G.B. shook his head.

"Good point," Law replied. "Well get this dumbass apple seed planted, bruh. You good?"

"No. My lady is missin' and so is my unborn child," Bucks said. "Nobody gets mercy. Nobody."

His guys nodded their heads in agreement. They dapped and embraced Bucks before he went and hopped up into his SS and left.

***

Heading up 21st Street, he came to a stop sign at 21st and Kenosha Road when his phone rang.

"What up, though, bruh?" Bucks answered, seeing Javi was calling.

"Swing past my yard, my nigga," Javi told him.

"On the way," Bucks replied, ending the call, then he hit the gas and left Lexani tire rubber on the ground when all 750 horsepower under the MC's hood launched it forward like it was flung from a slingshot.

Chapter 6

Bucks came up to Kilbourne Road and hit a right from Russell Road. He headed north up the two-way road as two big semi-trucks rolled past him in the opposite direction. One of them honked as they passed him.

The entrance to Valdez Transport, LLC's entrance came up just after he passed the entrance to PJ&D Transport's big trucking yard. Bucks turned into Valdez Transport's yard and saw so many big rigs and trailers inside the one-acre lot that it looked like a commercial vehicle dealership. There were rows of trucks on one side, parked under bright lights, and at the rear, rows of various kinds of trailers. Bucks was always amazed when he went to Javi's trucking company. The green-eyed Dominicano was so rich it was ridiculous. He owned eighty trucks and close to one hundred trailers. The cheapest vehicle in Javi's fleet was no less than seventy thousand.

***

At the big office building, which was connected to a long, tall diesel maintenance garage, Bucks saw Javi and his wife, both standing next to an enormous Hennessey Performance-edition Dodge Ram Mammoth 6x6 pickup truck, looking like a giant black mini monster truck, sitting on six big off-road wheels instead of just four. Javi and his wife were both in all-black, hooded up, looking like they were ready to go hit a lick.

Bucks rolled up and parked next to the massive pick-up truck. He hopped out and dapped Javi, then gave Michelle a hug.

"Everything aight?" he then asked.

"Sort of. Wonderin' if you got time to take a ride with' bae and me? We gots to go huntin' for dummies," Javi said.

Michelle chuckled. "Super dumb dummies," she added.

"Sheit, y'all already know I'm wit' the shit. Let's ride, Joe."

Javi nodded. "Hop in. Pick yo' tool, too. I'm sure you'll find what works under the backseat."

They hopped up inside the Ram's exclusive blacked-out cab. Javi started the racing-built supercharged V8 under the hood, so powerful that it shook the truck.

"Oh, shit! Daayuum, Joe!" Bucks eyes went wide when he saw what was under the seat. "Y'all got some serious pull to have one of these muthafuckas!"

"It pays to have ex-military people in the family that still have connections," Michelle said, as she pulled two custom Glock 18s up from by her feet, both with mini-100-round drums locked in.

Bucks could see that Javi and Michelle were most definitely on that with whoever. Riding on 'eights, thumped up like it was legal, Bucks felt like he was right at home. Javie turned out of his yard onto Kilbourne and hit the gas, opening up 1,012 horsepower in an instant. Michelle reached over to the dash and turned the music up. The Ruff Ryders' "Jigga" with Jay-Z started bumping from the woofers in the rear that Bucks didn't even know were there.

***

"Wow." T.G. shook his head, looking at the encrypted email sent to him by Samantha. He was instantly filled with affliction when he saw who the next person Samantha wanted knocked off. He wasn't sure he could stomach this one.

"What's wrong?"

T.G. looked up from his phone at Denise, across the table from him. At a twenty-four-hour Denny's Restaurant out in Waukegan's Lakehurst area, T.G. had decided to treat his guest to a big meal before going home for the night. He found that more and more he enjoyed being in Denise and Letoya's company. They made him feel a sense of responsibility that made him feel like the Man above was giving him to absolve his dark soul of the foul way that he had done Yvette and Julie.

"Hello? Tremaine?" Denise waved her fork with a pancake slice in it at him. He blinked his eyes coming out of his daze.

"My bad. What did you say?"

"You said, 'Wow,' like you got some bad news on yo' phone. I was just askin' if you were okay?"

T.G. sighed. "Not in any way shape or form, but eventually I will be," he told her. "How's lil' mama doin'?" he then asked, unable to see Letoya in her baby carrier.

"Sleepin'. I'm jealous."

T.G. chuckled. "Well, let's finish up and get home so y'all can get some rest."

"We," Denise corrected.

"Huh?" His eyebrows furrowed.

"You look like yo' ass ain't slept in days. You can forget about handlin' any more business 'til I think you are fully rested, sir."

"Oh, you the boss of me now?" T.G. asked, as she ate her slice.

"Naw, but a good woman never lets a good man make moves if he ain't operatin' at one hunnid percent."

T.G. eyebrows slightly rose up. That shocked him, hearing her taking charge, wanting him to be ready for whatever he may face on his next job, like a ride or die chick does for her man.

He nodded his head lost for words at the moment. She was growing on him, little by little, every minute he was with her. Denise was truly beautiful in so many ways, inside and out. She was different from Yvette. Denise was hood, but she was the type of hood chick that needed to be protected and held. Yvette protected herself, and she held herself. Denise was like the singer Saweetie, while Yvette was like GloRilla. Couldn't go wrong with either of them, but they were both very different, in every way.

"Glad we got that understood," Denise said, grabbing her cup of apple juice and taking a sip. "And from this moment on, I'm gonna make sure you are in tip top shape, before you got to make moves."

"It's cool. Denise, I'ma be—"

"What I say?" she shot back, cutting him off.

Taken aback by her aggressiveness, T.G. couldn't help but cheese up.

Maybe she ain't that much different from Yvette, mentally, but one thing's for sure...lil' mama makin' me wanna see if she taste as good as she looks, T.G. thought, smiling at her.

Yeah, nigga. I see you lookin' wit' cho lookin' ass, knowin' you can tell when a real-ass ride or die bitch is in yo' presence, you sexy muthafucka you, Denise thought, smiling back at him. They both held each other's gaze for a minute, before T.G. threw his hands up in surrender.

"You win," he told her, knowing exactly how determined and bossy a black woman could be.

***

"Ooohhh! Yeah! Ooooo, God! Yees!" cried Samantha, her back arching as he dined on her, pleasing her body, making her head feel like it was about to explode. "Oh my God, Dale! Holy shit! Oohhh, G-G-Gooooood!"

She climaxed so hard seconds later, splashing his face, drenching it. She went limp on their bed, astounded that her husband had actually made her cum.

"Not talkin' shit now, eh, you little cunt?" Webster asked as he climbed his naked frame on top of her. Samantha's phone rang as he made her open her legs for him.

"What are you doing, Sammie? We're having sex, dammit!" he snapped when she reached for her phone. She grabbed it from the nightstand, ignoring him and answered it.

"I'm a little busy right now, so this better be important."

"It is! Why are you screwing with them?" Samantha heard Bernice demand to know. "I came back from Aruba and I see all hell's broken loose!"

Samantha chuckled, looking up at her frowning husband.

"It's lovely, isn't it? Soon, all will be revealed," Samantha said.

"What did you do with the girls?" Bernice asked.

"Wouldn't you like to know."

Bernice cursed. "You're gonna sink our ship, you dumb horny hoe."

"Takes one to know one, cunt! Buh-bye now!"

Samantha ended the call. "Okay, now where were we, honey?"

"You were about to suck my cock since you made me lose my boner," Webster told her.

"Ha! In your dreams, player. Nice try, now get off of me and don't come back 'til you got three Viagras in you and a shot of Jimmy Beam. Buh-bye, now!"

Webster curled his lip up at his wife, but got off her, muttering a curse as he headed towards the bathroom. As soon as the door shut, Samantha jumped up and hurried to put her lace bra and panties on, her long-sleeved wrap-dress, her knee-high stiletto boots. She grabbed her phone, keys to her M3 then snuck out to go get some of the best dick she ever had in her life.

***

"Orale, Guey! Feliz Cumpleaños, Cabrón," shouted Gallo, holding up his Dos Equis in salute to the boss.

Just over ninety other men and women followed suit. Dressed in expensive clothing, wearing expensive jewelry, liquored up, coked out, the big group of members of the Serrano Cartel were all out to celebrate the 59th birthday of Felix Reyes-Serrano. The man was gettin on in his years. His top capos were all itching to take over when he stepped down, which included his two sons and his daughter.

In a gigantic mansion that sat on two acres of land, out of the edge of Lake County's Grayslake area, the birthday bash was live and filled with celebratory vibes. Felix had been warring with other Mexican cartels, a Colombian cartel and a big Dominican family. Recently, in attempts to really show people that the Serrano Cartel was not some punk-ass street clique, Felix had ordered a hit-crew to advance on one of the Valdez family's chemical producing plants. It was a city-sized business down in Joliet, that made hundreds of millions of dollars per month for Juan and Diego Valdez, the two younger brothers of the deceased Pedro Valdez, who had started what was a multi-billion-dollar empire of business, and cocaine importing/distribution.

There were so many casualties and so much destruction that Felix just knew the Dominican would think twice about screwing with him, packing up, and taking their asses back to the East Coast.

***

"Papi! Dios Mio! I love you so much," exclaimed Felix's daughter Jehida, hugging and kissing her father's cheek while her younger brothers, Pico and Paco stood to the side, despising how much their big-breasted sister kissed ass.

"Ay, mija, tambien yo te quiero mucho," Felix replied, hugging Jehida back. "Pero, next time wear more appropriate clothes."

The young sexy brown Chicana wore a nude-colored Carolina Herrera dress that was so tight, it looked like she wasn't even wearing anything at all, since it matched her flawless skin. The sides were cut, revealing that she couldn't have been wearing a bra, nor any panties. The hem was so short if she didn't immediately cross her legs when she sat down, or if she bent over even a little, everyone that was looking would see the goodness graciousness she was barely hiding in her nude-colored fishnet pantyhose.

Her long silk golden hair matched the spike toe Christian Louboutins on her feet, and the gold jewelry that dripped all over her. The makeup she had on made Felix see a beauty pageant whore instead of his nineteen-year-old daughter.

"Daddy, we've been through this before," Jehida said to him, with a devious smile. "I'm a grown woman, blessed with beauty. There is nothing wrong with showing off a little."

Felix knew he was not going to win. His daughter had dug her pricey heels in, and not even a mule could pull her free. Pico and Paco walked up, both of the seventeen-year-old fraternal twins towering over sis and pops. They embraced their father with hugs while dying to know who would take over for him when he stepped down. They were ready to kill anyone for the power, but unbeknownst to them, so was big sis.

"I'm going to use the ladies' room," Jehida said, giving her brothers a sly glance, before walking off, switching her larger-than average culo hard for all the eyes she knew were eye-fucking her.

"Pinche whore," Pico muttered, seeing Jehida give a flirtatious wave and smile to Gallo, who had given it right back to her. Paco shook his head. He hated the forty-seven-year-old with a passion not just because Gallo was fucking his barely legal sister, allegedly, but because everyone was sure that Gallo would be who Felix chose to succeed him.

***

Jehida hurried through the marble hallway from the grand ballroom of her father's house. Her Red Bottom heels clacked loudly on the floor. She turned her head, looking at the tall glazed French hardwood doors she had just come through. Nobody followed. Jehida put a little pep in her step and got to the last door on her right. She entered a security code in the pas lock at the side of the door, then hurried into the big champagne room.

Racks with chilled bottles of Ace, Dom, Belaire and Moet lined the walls. Jehida went to one where a rack with limited edition Moet bottles were in cases. She grabbed a bottle of Moet out and under it, took the laser emitting key tucked away there, and went to what looked like a plain concrete wall. Holding the key to a pot in the corner that looked like it was a coffee stain, she heard the mechanical components inside working. The hi-tech security lock opened up, then the wall started sliding to the right, revealing the stairway to the underground escape tunnel.

There on the other side was the big muscular Dominican, the most amazingly handsome man Jehida had ever met. She was gone over his big muscles, his GQ-handsome face, his crisp bald-fade haircut with the curls-for-the-girls on top, and his deep rich cocoa-complexioned skin tone. He was a six-foot-three-inch masterpiece in her eyes, with money longer than hers, and a phenomenal sex game.

"Heey, papi chulo," Jehida purred, loving how thuggish he looked in black Timbs, black jeans, the black hoodie, and a Chicago Bulls fitted. "You look so good right now."

Xavier Valdez chuckled at the starry-eyed look in the Chicana's eyes.

"Why thank you, lil' mama, had to dress for the occasion."

"Ahem! Hello! Move yo' big ass out the way, nigga!"

Jehida craned her neck and looked behind her Afro-Latino stud. There waiting for him to step in, Jehida saw his wild-ass sister Evelyn, his sister's lesbian lover Gloria, along with his older but smaller green-eyed brother Javi, Javi's wife Michelle, and another tall light-skinned guy that she didn't know.

"No need to be rude, Eve," Jehida said to the Valdez family princess, rolling her eyes.

Jehida took Xavier's hand and pulled him in. The others entered, all of them with deadly automatic weapons, two with machetes hooked to their sides.

"So, once the old bastard is gone, I'll take over the Serrano Cartel," Jehida said to the Valdez family goons. "And at that point, I will make you…" pausing to look at Xavier, with a smile, "my main supplier."

"Sounds good to me, mamita," he replied, with a smile of his own.

"There's just one problem, though, Jehida," she heard Michelle say.

Turning and facing the Dominicana, she raised an eyebrow.

"And what problem would that be, Michelle?" she asked sassily.

CRACK

Evelyn cocked back and fired Jehida's jaw up, sending her to the floor seeing two of everything.

"What the hell, you crazy bitch?" Jehida cried, jaw and head throbbing as she looked up, trying to narrow down which Evelyn was real, and which was not.

She was then grabbed by her hair and yanked up from the floor. She screamed in pain until a hand came flying and smacked the shit out of her. Michelle appeared in front of her. "The problem is, bitch, is that we don't fuck with snakes, and anybody that will let the opps into their family's home to kill them, is the biggest snake in the world."

"And you know what they say," she heard Evelyn then say. The person holding her up by her hair turned her to face Evelyn. Jehida saw her gripping her machete like it was a baseball bat.

"You chop the head off of a snake, the baby dies."

***

Bucks saw Gloria let go of Jehida. The Mexican screamed. Evelyn swung the machete.

WHACK

Jehida's head went flying after it was severed from her body. Her body hit the floor, blood spurting out of the stump, head landing by the rack with Dom on it, eyes sill open in fear. Chuckling, Bucks said, "It never ceases to amaze me how true it is what they say about y'all, when the Valdez family comes, head roll."

Javi, his wife and the others laughed.

"We got plenty more to do, my boy," Xavier said then.

"Let's get to it," Javi added.

He and Bucks went and grabbed the metal carry cases that sat just on the other side of the escape tunnel's hideaway wall, then with the layout of the Serrano mansion in Xavier's head, he led the way for them to get in position, while the others that had just arrived to join the party get in their positions as well.

Bucks was super geeked to once again be on a mission with such a dynasty of a family. Riding with Javi and his people was as good as it got to him. The benefits that came from loyalty were one thing, but overall, it was just fun as fuck to him.

Chapter 7

T.G. jumped when he heard knocking on the door. Denise woke up, having fallen asleep on the couch next to him, where they were watching the devastating news of Chicago rapper Lil' Durk being booked for alleged murder-for-hire charges.

Denise saw it was 2:30 am. She furrowed her eyebrow, opening her mouth to speak when suddenly, T.G.'s hand flew over her mouth, stopping her.

"Do not make a sound," he whispered, as three more knocks came. "Hurry up and get to Letoya, go into the spot that I showed you, and do not come out until you hear me make the signal noise. Go!"

Denise rose up from the couch.

"Tremaine! Open up!"

They heard Samantha's voice. Denise half wanted to run to the door, snatch it open and beat the bitch up until she pissed herself, but Samantha was way to connected, and she knew her baby's life would be in even more danger than it already was.

She reluctantly hurried off, running barefoot to get her little girl, and to hide in the secret secure room T.G. told her that nobody but he knew about.

"Tremaaaiiine!"

T.G. got up and went to open the door. Samantha stood there, looking frustrated but sexy as hell in a MILF-type dress and high-heeled boots with her long tresses hanging loose down her shoulders.

"What took you so damn long? I hate waiting!" she snapped, pushing past him like she was welcomed in. T.G. shook his head, closing and locking the door. He turned to her and saw her go by the couch.

"Is there somethin' you need? I was sleepin'," he told her, making his way towards her. Samantha's eye momentarily looked at the TV. The former Bad Boys mogul was on the news, again being made to look like a horrible monster before he had his day in the court of law, when the video of what he did to his ex-girlfriend in a hotel hallway was played again.

She shook her head. "I hope they cook his ass, girls and boys? Sick bastard."

"Hello? Care to tell me what you poppin' up at my crib at 2:30 in the mornin' for?"

Samantha turned her head and looked at him. She smiled and closed the gap between them. She reached out and grabbed T.G.'s crotch, instantly growing aroused by how big and thick it was.

"Does that answer your question, big guy?"

T.G. chuckled. "Your husband know you're here?"

"He's at home, cursing me out for leaving him hanging with a Viagra-stiff rock?" Samantha let go of his hardening piece and untied the strap to her dress. Stepping back, she opened it up and let T.G. get a good look at her, in her Victoria's Secrets. "And if he knew I left his wrinkled white-ass for a big Black dick, he'd be pissed. That makes my pussy soooo wet!"

T.G. undid his pants and dropped them. His ten inches stood erect, painting right at her.

"You want this dick? Come suck on it first, then I'll give it to you like yo' bitch ass husband can't."

"Ooooo! I love it when you talk slick to me!" Samantha told him. She ran to him, dropped down and parted her classic red lips, opening her mouth wide for him. T.G. grinned. Holding his joint at the base, he stuffed his cock into her mouth, and his eyes rolled to the back of his head from the warm, wet, and skilled feeling of Samantha's mouth, as she wrapped her lips around his dick and started sucking.

***

Denise rocked back and forth worried sick about T.G. She had no clue why Samantha had popped up unannounced, but it couldn't be for anything good. *She found out I'm alive! Fuck! She probably came to kill him! I have to save him!* she thought, panicking with fear.

She looked over at her daughter. Letoya was sleeping peacefully in the crib that T.G. had built inside of the safe room. Denise went to the crib, leaned in, and kissed her baby's forehead.

"Mommy loves you, Letoya. But I can't let that bitch hurt him, if it wasn't for T.G., Mommy would be dead."

Denise hurried and grabbed the Draco that T.G. showed her how to shoot earlier that day and made her way to go rescue him and murder the conniving bitch before she could murder T.G.

***

What the fuck? Oh, heeeell no! This nigga 'dun lost his mind! Denise thought, jaw dropped eyes wide with shock once she saw T.G. sitting on the couch and Samantha on her knees in front of him, sucking the shit out of his dick. She heard T.G. groaning and cursing as the white woman pleased him. She heard Samantha sucking and slurping loudly, moaning and giggling like she was having the time of her life.

Fury struck Denise like a pimp slapping his bitch for backtalking him. She saw red. Before she knew it, she was pointing the AK-47 pistol at Samantha's back. Right as her finger wrapped around the trigger, she caught sight of T.G.'s hand motioning for her attention. She saw him looking her way, face contorted, but clearly forbidding her to shoot. He shook his head no, then his eyes rolled to the back of his head. Denise grinded her teeth in anger but fell back. She quietly bent back around the corner, disappearing from his line of sight.

***

"Fuck! Goddamn, bitch! Wooo!" he shouted, as Samantha went bananas on him. She spit his dick out when it started pulsating in her mouth. Tasting pre-cum, Samantha knew he wasn't far off. She wanted to cum too, so she stood, pulled her dress all the way off, undid her bra and dropped her panties. She climbed onto T.G.'s lap, mounting him. She slid down on his throbbing cock, filling herself up with Black bliss. She bit her bottom lip as his size gave her such euphoric pleasure. Her head went back and she moaned out at the top of her lungs, thinking that it was only her and T.G. in the house.

***

Denise peeked back around the corner and saw Samantha riding T.G.'s dick. The way the woman was moaning made Denise jealous that she contemplated saying what T.G. said, pop that bitch in the back of her head, then take her place on top of T.G. She watched the white woman bounce up and down. They both moaned, groaned, cursing repeatedly. Then Samantha cried out even louder. Denise could tell that she had just climaxed. *Lucky bitch!* Denise thought, as Samantha hopped off T.G.'s dick, put her hands on the couch, bending all the way over.

T.G. smacked Samantha's ass hard, making her shriek from the sting. She leaned her face down to the couch cushion, reached back and grabbed her ass cheeks, opening them up for T.G. He spit a wad of saliva onto her puckered brown-eye then gripping his cock, he put his bulbous tip to it, smeared it all around, then started easing it inside of her asshole.

Denise listed to Samantha curse and talk shit while she looked back at T.G. Her pussy dripping wet, hearing the slapping skin, the bitch going crazy as T.G. cracked her. Denise absentmindedly slipped a hand down into her leggings, into her panties, and started playing with her pussy. She kept her eyes on the two, mostly on T.G.'s backside.

Her breathing grew labored. Her temperature rose. Her body craved release. She bit her bottom lip to keep quiet. Her fingers worked her clit. Her knees shook, T.G. filled her mind, looking so good as her own little fantasy ran vividly through her mind.

***

"Oooooooohhhh, sshhiiiiit! Yeeess!" Samantha screamed out at the top of her lungs. Then she exploded all over T.G.'s legs. He kept on fucking her ass until he felt his nut rising up. Quickly, he pulled his dick out and started stroking himself until he exploded nutting all over her booty cheeks. He coated them with globs of hot semen. Samantha moaned, feeling the droplets on her skin. She sat upright, turned and bent down, taking his dick in her hand and running her tongue up the tip, slurping up the last of his jizz.

"You's a nasty bitch," T.G. said to her, turned on and repulsed by the traitorous slut.

Samantha swallowed it, stood back up, and smiled at him.

"And dangerous, too," she told him.

Minutes later she was dressed and out the door, switching her ass like she just knew T.G. was looking.

***

"That bitch is cray-cray," T.G. said to himself, as he pulled his boxers and pants back up.

"Ooo!"

He heard her just then. Eyes buggin wide open, T.G. made his way to where Denise had been about to shoot the shit out of Samantha. He found the sexy chocolate queen up against the wall, looking like she had just gotten caught with her hand in the cookie jar...literally.

"Uh...you good?" he asked, looking at her with furrowed brows.

Denise looked at him with big, startled eyes and a wet hand.

"Y-yeah...why wouldn't I be?"

"Because you're posted here and I just heard you...moan...or scream...whatever the hell that was."

She smacked her lips. "Nigga, mind yo business!"

Denise grabbed the Draco from the floor and rushed off, back to her child before she got even more tempted to jump T.G.'s bones and remind him how good Black pussy was.

***

Felix sat at the long table, clothed with a ruby-colored velvet tablecloth. All sorts of Mexican delicacies were on plates and bowls. Bottles lined up chilled and ready to pour, with the top dogs of Felix's main circle, ready to get slapped. Pico and Paco sat at their pop's left and Gallo was to his boss's right. Felix was enjoying himself but kept wondering what was taking his daughter so long.

"Where is Jehida?" he asked Paco.

"No se, Papa," Paco shrugged.

"I'll go get her, Patron," Gallo offered, all too willing to catch his young freak in the bathroom and fuck her again, for the third time since she put on her booty-hugging dress.

"We should kill him first," Pico said to his brother, as they both watched Gallo head towards the big French doors that led out of the ballroom to the hallway where the bathroom was.

"In time, bro, be patient," Paco replied.

BOOOM!

The second Paco finished his statement a huge explosion rocked the whole ballroom. A big ball of fire exploded from the French doors engulfing Gallo, instantly vaporizing him. People that had been close to the doors were fried and sent flying. Pico, Paco, and Felix jumped up from their seat, eyes bugged wide open, tripping hard.

From the obliterated doorway to the hall, dark smoke came billowing, while flames consumed the walls and the dead bodies lay out on the floor.

"Oye, Serrano putas! Here comes the Dominicanoos! Ayayayayaaaa, muthafuckaaaa!" Everyone shouted from the smoke. A missile was then shot into the ballroom, hitting a heavy-set man. While he was blown to pieces, the large group that had been with him were tuned into crispy fried chunks of meat.

Bucks and Javi dropped their spent hand-held rocket launchers and grabbed the AK-47's that were suspended by shoulder straps around their necks.

"Vamos!" Javi hollered to his people.

They ran into the ballroom, entering chaos, dumping at everyone moving. Bucks took aim at a crowd of security and shot left, right, left, sweeping side to side like an expert annihilator.

BRRRRRRRRRRRRRRRRRRRRR!

He squeezed again at another mob of armed men that he peeped running up to the banister at the upper section of the ballroom, dropping them with ease.

Javi and his wife fanned down a few fleeing cartel members. Xavier, Evelyn, and Gloria blew down those they knew were accountants and money launderers for the Serrano Cartel.

BOC! BOC! BOC! BOC! BOC! BOC!

"AAGGHH!"

Bucks felt the hot string of a bullet slam into his chest. It pushed him backwards. He hit the floor hard, feeling like his chest had been broken. A shooter ran up on him with an MP5 and pointed it right at his face.

BRRRRRRRRRRRRRRRRR!

BRRRRRRRRRRRRRRRRR!

Michelle hit the guy from ten feet away, filling him with so many rounds that he was nearly cut in half. Javi grabbed Bucks by the hand and pulled him up.

"It ain't break time yet, my nigga!" he hollered jokingly over all the gunfire.

Just then, he saw Javi's eyes avert away from him. He turned and saw two young boys shouting at Xavier, Evelyn, and Gloria, while they ran behind an older man covering him.

"Aye! That's them!" Bucks shouted, ready to finish the job, despite how much his chest hurt.

"Hold up, hold up, hold up," Javi halted him as his wife popped the very last of the Serrano Cartel hitters, blowing a hole through his chest that looked like a cannon ball went through him. "Relax, bruh. They aren't goin' nowhere." Bucks watched the leader of the cartel and his sons run out of a door, disappearing from sight.

***

"Hijole de la chingada!" Felix shouted when he and his boys made it out of the burning house. Pico and Paco gasped when they saw nineteen men and women, standing in a line, thumped up with big choppers, looking like a firing squad. They weren't alone. In front of them, eighteen dogs, Rottweilers, Pit Bulls, a Presa Camario, a Cane Corso, a

Dego Argentino and the nineteenth meat-eating animal, a full-grown snow leopard.

The three nearly shitted on themselves. They attempted to run back to the house, only to run into the party crashers as they all came out of the same door that the three had just come out of.

***

BRRRRRRRRR!

Bucks pointed his chopper at Pico and blew him to pieces. Javi turned Paco's lights out. Felix remained, with a big wet spot at the crotch of his tuxedo. Bucks saw one of the old heads of the Valdez family step out from the line. He had only seen pictures of the seventy-three-year-old, fair-skinned Dominican, but he knew that it was Juanito Valdez, the former second-in-command of the multi-billion-dollar cocaine importing and trafficking organization that he and his younger brother's older deceased brother started from the mud, nearly fifty years ago.

His wife, Carolina, was at Juanito's side. Diego, Juanito's ox-built little brother, and Diego's wife Maritza along with Larissa, the widow of Pedro Valdez, all stepped towards Felix Serrano, with their dogs at their sides.

"Oooooo, they finna beat that bitch ass nigga's ass, bro!" Bucks heard Macho, the wild one of the Valdez family, say to his older brother Tool.

The two Pittsburgh, PA native, dread head Dominericans wore yellow Terrible Towel bandanas on their necks, as did their older cousin Danny, king of the family and the five other members of the Steel City Mafia City, the twins Cee and Dee, Perry and the first and only lady of the SCM, Lacy. Macho's wife, Yessinia and Danny's wife, ChaCha, had New York Jets bandanas around their necks, while Macho's Chicago-born girlfriend rocked a Bears bandana around her neck.

The last two, Jamaica, head of the Valdez family's massive army of Caribbean Killers, and his right hand, Gold Mouth, were a big part of the family. The Rasta Gangsters had lost people close to them when Felix's goons hit up Juanito and Diego's chemical plant. Felix knees trembled as he looked into the angry eyes of the four old school Dominicanos.

Buck actually felt bad for the man. He pitied Felix, but in no way shape or form planned to not watch the man die.

"Por favor, no me mates!"

Juanito dug into the pocket of his black cargo pants and pulled out a little pill. Then Diego rushed in and socked Felix so hard that his jawbone shattered. He flew backwards and hit the ground. The old Chicano cried in pain, holding his broken jaw. Carolina crouched down next to him, grabbed his mouth and pried it open, causing lightning jolts of pain to strike Felix. Juanito dropped the pill into Felix's mouth, then Carolina forced it back closed, delivering a karate-chop to his throat, which made Felix swallow the pill. Her husband took her hand and helped her back up. "Mataste a mi gente, mamahuevo!" Juanito's powerfully deep voice boomed angrily. "Gente que eran buen trabajadoras y mantenían a sus familias, bitch! Por eso, vas a moril!"

Bucks had no clue what the old Dominican said, but right after he had spoken, Felix started shaking and groaning in agony. He grabbed his throat. The color of his brown skin flushed, and his being began popping out as if he was mutating. They all watched Felix Serrano burn to death from the inside out. The radiation pill that had been forced down his throat worked like he had eaten a torch. He fried from the inside, his skin turning red, then darkening. Bucks' jaw dropped as he continued watching the paisano's skin blacken. He convulsed and his eyes rolled so far to the back of his head that only the whites showed. Seconds later, a puff of smoke came out of Felix's mouth, then he went still.

"Whoa." Bucks was beyond thrilled. He looked at Javi. "That was some shit niggas only see in Steven King movies, Joe."

"Yeah. My cousin Macho ain't the only crazy nigga in the family. He hails from crazy," Javi said.

"Better believe it!" Macho hollered, as they all made their way to where five black Bell 505 helicopters sat next to Javi's Hennessey Ram and Xavier's big stupid Ford F-250 Mega Rexx pick-up truck.

"Aye, Joe! Next time, don't nobody need all that black 'n yellow to come blow clowns down either, cuz!" Javi said, reaching the passenger door of his Ram.

"Nigga, stop," Macho replied, holding his wife Yessina's hand as she got up in the pilot's seat, with his girlfriend G-Baby climbing in next, then their snow leopard Sky, their Rottweiler Maliante, and their Red Nose Pit, Dreams. "Don't be mad 'cause ya bitch ass Bears lost to a tipped-ass Hail Mary! Bear down, nigga!"

"Javier! Get cha' ass in so we can go, dammit!" Michelle yelled at her husband, before the two brother-looking cousins started arm-wrestling.

"This ain't over, foo'!" Javi said, climbing up inside.

"Yes, it is, muthafuckaa!" Macho hollered over the loud helicopter rotor blades spinning. "Pittsburgh is gon' crush the little punk-ass Giants!"

"I'ma smack ya cousin, yo," Michelle said, flooring it away from the mansion, with Xavier behind her, while the helicopters all lifted off into the pitch-black sky. "Talkin' shit about my ten 'n shit."

"I thought you was a Jets fan, bae?" Javier asked her.

"I'm a fan of anything New York, boo-boo. New York runs it while Chicago fumbles it."

"Come on now. Green Bay is gon' take it all this year, Joe."

Javi looked back at him. Michelle glanced at him in the mirror, right as she flew through the gate that Javi ran through on the way in.

"Bro, you's a rider, and I got mad love for you, but if you bring up them cheese turds in this vehicle again, we gon' drop you off at the Greyhound Station and see you later," Javi said.

Bucks busted out laughing at his homeboy.

Chapter 8

Early the next morning, T.G. prepared himself to head out. Dressed and ready to go on probably the most gut-wrenching job he was sure Samantha would throw at him, T.G. stood in front of the full-length mirror in his bedroom and took a long hard look at himself. He shook his head.

"Him? Al all people? Why?" T.G. asked himself, perturbed in the worst way about the job. Taking a deep breath then exhaling, he grabbed his duffle bag, and made his way out of his room, making a pit-stop by Denise's room.

Cuddled in the covers, Denise was sleeping peacefully. T.G. smiled at the sight of how peaceful she looked. He then heard Letoya giggling. Walking to her crib, he peered in at the little girl. She was wide awake, arms flailing, legs kicking, giggling at the stuffed Minnie Mouse doll next to her. Her head turned and up she looked at T.G. Letoya smiled at him and started kicking her little legs more.

Smiling brighter, T.G. set the bags down, reached in and gently picked her up. He carried her to the rocker in the corner and sat with her.

"Hey there, pretty little lady. Why ain't you sleepin' huh?" he cooed softly to her, holding her head steady with one hand, while the other held her up by her back. Letoya started blowing spit bubbles while she laughed. T.G. felt a fatherly instinct inside of him. He felt the need to care for, and to protect the helpless infant, with his life.

***

Denise opened her eyes when she heard T.G.'s voice and her daughter giggling happily. She saw him on the rocking chair holding Letoya lovingly, like a proud father. She could hear him talking to Letoya, saying some of the sweetest things about her, and about her daughter.

"I promise you, little lady, you and mommy will be safe with me. I will protect you both, and I will make sure you both live as great a life as possible."

Denise eyes filled with tears from his words. She was listening to a man. A man that had a heart and truly cared for her and her child. She continued to watch, not moving, just observing.

T.G. planted a soft kiss on Letoya's forehead. He rose up, and gently laid her back in her crib, placing her so that she could roll, but not end up on her face, and end up suffocating.

Turning to leave after he scooted her Minnie Mouse a little closer to her hands, T.G. started towards the bedroom doorway.

"Tremaine?"

He paused, hearing Denise call to him. Turning towards her, he saw her getting up from the bed, wearing just a big t-shirt that he knew was his. Denise walked up to him. She reached up and grabbed him by the collar of his hoodie, and pulled him down to her, then she pressed her lips to his.

T.G. was astounded by her move. Her lips were so soft and her sensualness moved him. She kissed him passionately, with excitement. He felt himself wishing the kiss was never ending. She pulled back a minute later. Feeling all tingly, inside, Denise smiled up at him.

"Se pou Bondye fe' ou tounen vin jwenn nou an sekirite," she said.

T.G.'s eyebrow furrowed. "What in the hell did you just say?"

She chuckled. "It's Haitian Creole. I said, "May God bring you back to us safely."

"Oh…well, thank you. You speak that shit fluently?"

Denise nodded. "My mom and dad were born and raised in Port Au Prince, but they had me when they migrated to Flint, Michigan."

"Damn, Denise. You just get better and better to me," T.G. told her, amazed all over again by the beautiful mother. She smiled harder at that.

"I'll be back. How about a trip when I return?" T.G. suggested, knowing that after the job was done, he himself would need a vacation.

"Sounds good to me. We'll be ready to go when you get here. "

T.G. nodded his head, then kissing her lips again he headed out, leaving Denise feeling like she was floating on a cloud.

***

Bucks stood in front of the grave of Brandon Harris, aka Twist. The eighteen-year-old dope boy had not made it to his nineteenth year of life. He had met his demise when he and his three homies chose a hood belonging to the Maniac Latin Disciples of Wauk-Town, to dump off some coke that Bucks and T.G. put them on with.

"I'm sorry, lil' Lord," Bucks said, as he remembered the young Conservative Vicelord, and how thorough he was about getting that bag. Bucks and T.G. had handled those responsible for Twist's death, and the serious injuries his Lord homies sustained by the 'Yaks. Bucks was grateful that they were still alive, but had forbidden them to move amongst the streets anymore. They now were employed at his exotic/foreign dealership and were enrolled in one of the most prestigious mechanic schools in the state of Illinois.

"You will never be forgotten, fam. On God," Bucks swore. He then sighed. Two and half million dollars had been put out on T.G.'s head. So many eyes were looking for him, but not a single sighting of him had been reported. Shaking his head, Bucks walked off from Twist's headstone. He went and hopped into his restored 1967 Pontiac GTO and fired up the big 400-cubic-inch V8 under the hood. He pulled off and got on his way to check up on the construction of one of his newest businesses that he had created without T.G.'s name being associated with his.

***

Lieutenant Michaels shook his head. The sight in front of him was truly gruesome but in all his years on the force, he had seen enough to give Dick Wolf enough material to create another cop TV show. The bodies of three little girls, their parents and their grandparents were all tied up, mouths covered with duct tape, and bullet holes in their foreheads, had the veteran state police lieutenant close to tears. The girls were all under ten years old, and the grandparents were in their eighties.

From the detectives that were on the scene, a truck stop along Interstate 294 in Northbrook, the big expensive motorcoach RV bus the Hispanic family had been en route to take a trip to Mexico in from the father's million-dollar home up in Vernon Hills. The camera at the corners of the diesel fuel station caught a caravan of masked men, surmised to be Sicarios, overtook the big Pevost and turned the inside into a bloody horror film scene. Furthermore, it was discovered that the father was part of a rival cartel, acting as a money laundering accountant. He had bags of cash in the compartments of his bus, and the camera revealed that after the Sicarios had been on the bus for nearly half an hour, the nine hitters hurried out of the bus, all of them carrying bags that looked very heavy.

A whole twenty-five minutes passed before the first state police vehicle arrived on scene. Nobody had heard a single gunshot. The Sicarios had silenced guns.

***

"We've got plate numbers on the vehicles the suspects were in, Lieutenant," said a junior state police detective, a young ambitious Black woman that reminded Michaels of Yvette, when she first joined the state police department, with Julie, fresh from the Waukegan Police Department. "Unfortunately, every one of them were reported stolen a week ago and as of an hour ago, they were found down in Chicago in the Back of the Yard, burned to crisps."

"So, no prints, hair, nor any other DNA of any kind." Michaels already knew.

She shook her head. "Sorry, sir."

"There's no reason to apologize, Detective Dover. Good work, keep your eyes fresh on this one. Those children and those old-timers didn't deserve to go like that because of the father living on the wrong side.

"His wife was in on it. She established businesses with money he constantly added to his bank account."

Michaels looked at Dover. "Are you saying that Mr. Florez was possibly stealing from whoever he worked for?"

"It seems like that to me, sir. He has absolutely no known ties to the Olivarez Cartels, so it's not likely any of their enemies would know who he is, right easy. The money he launders, there are reports that he's been in hot water with the bosses in the past, over theft allegations, but he always somehow proved his innocence, then someone else died."

Michaels shook his head again. "He was very dirty."

"That would be my guess, and it's finally caught up to him," said Dover.

After a few more detectives brought Michaels their findings, he headed to his department-issued Expedition. As he was climbing in, he heard his name being hollered. Looking towards the crowds of his subordinates he saw his good friend, Lieutenant Walter Sikes, walking towards him with his three-year-old Belgian Malinois Ranger, on a leash.

"Hell of a scene here, eh?" the tall white man with a reddish-brown beard, in his late thirties said to Michaels, with a look of sorrow etched on his face.

"Yes, it is, Sikes. I'd love to find the pricks that did this shit, but that's like going searching for a Latino in Latin America."

Lieutenant Sikes nodded in agreement. "Can't wait to see what happens if they let that punk back into the White House, nor can I wait to see what Kamala does when she gets in."

Michaels looked at Sikes.

"You sound real confident that she's gonna win." Sikes grinned.

"Jarvis, let's be real about this. On our crazy planet, there are a lot of things that are either unbreakable, unchallengeable, indisputable, but what will always and forever be unbeatable, is a Black woman with a mission. Isn't that right, Ranger?"

Sikes' dog barked three times, wagging his tail excitedly. Michaels chuckled, mostly because he knew it was true. Out of all the faces in the world, nobody, absolutely nobody, could deny that a determined woman, especially a Black woman, got what she wanted, every time.

"Any word on the Samantha chick?" Sikes asked, then Michaels shook his head.

"She hides in plain sight, trust and believe, though... I will find out who she is, and her damn friend."

Sikes nodded. "Jones? Tran?"

Again, Michaels shook his head. "I still believe they are alive, Sikes. I feel like they're likely being held against their will. If Webster wanted them dead, they'd have been laid out at the gas station. Webster took 'em...he took Jones and Tran, and only he knows where they are."

"Then we dedicate every resource we have to finding him so that we can make him tell us where they are."

Michaels agreed. "I'll give Bucks a call 'n ask him to reach out to...them."

"Good thinking. Those people can find a needle in a pile of needles," Sikes said.

The two shook hands. Michaels patted Ranger's head, then climbing up into his SUV, he started his engine, put it in drive and pulled off, grabbing his phone from the center cup holder and giving Bucks a call.

***

"Talk to me, ol' man," Bucks answered.

"Can you ask your friends to shift gears and focus on Zack Morris?"

"I can."

"Good. Everything okay?" Michaels then asked.

"I mean no disrespect, sir, but that question is really pissin' me off. No. I am not okay, my pregnant fiancée and her best friend that is like a little sister to me, are in the hands of a fucking freak. I will not be okay until they're back and he's dead!"

Michaels came to a stop at a red light where a busy intersection teemed with traffic. Sitting in the right lane, he listened to Bucks. He was furious.

"I feel the same, youngster," Michaels replied.

Movement in his left peripheral caught his attention for a quick second. He froze when he saw the barrel of a big pistol pointed right at him from inside of a pick-up truck on his right, but when he saw whose hand it was in, Lieutenant Michael's jaw dropped.

***

T.G. gripped the Glock .40 tightly in his right hand, pointing it right at the lieutenant's face. His finger was wrapped around the trigger. His hand shook like he was freezing his ass off in Antarctica. The old man was frozen in place but looking dead at him. He knew that in a split second he was going to die. Gritting his teeth, T.G. tried to will himself to pull the trigger...but he couldn't. He couldn't make his finger work anymore than Lieutenant Michaels could unfreeze himself. Then a second later, the sounds of tires screeching got their attention. Up ahead, in the center of the big intersection, three windowless cargo vans had skidded to a stop, and mobs of Hispanics with big military guns jumped out.

"Oh, shit!" T.G. cussed, when they all pointed at the front of his stolen Chevy Silverado.

***

"Fuck!" Michaels gasped.

"What? What happened?" Bucks frantically asked.

Michaels dropped his phone and without thinking, he mashed the gas pedal down to the floor. His SUV shot forward, just as the group of nearly twenty hitters opened fire at T.G.

He swerved to the left, getting in front of T.G., using his own SUV as a shield. The shooters dove out of the way, nearly missing getting run over. Michaels gritted his teeth as bullets flew through his windshield. He ducked low as he got closer to the mob, preparing to make a hole, and hoped to God that T.G. was smart enough to follow.

***

"Get him! Get him!" Agarralo ese motherfucker!" Rueben yelled, sitting in the executive edition Cadillac Escalade ESU, in a corner of the parking lot, watching his mob of Sicarios that had just hopped out of the three vans and started dumping at the target.

Reuben, a young thuggish Columbian man was a top dog in the underworld of cocaine distribution. His older cousin Benicio had brought him into the game. Benicio had met his demise by a dirty cop that was connected to two beautiful lady cops that he had planned to continue to use on his side, as he took over for his dearly departed cousin.

Reuben had gotten a call from Yvette, informing him that she and Julie had the man responsible for Benicio's murder, and were bringing that man to him to be dealt with. But when she showed up with Julie and two men that he didn't know, Rueben discovered that Webster had flown the coop, and blamed Yvette and Julie. Adding fuel to the fire, T.G. had punched Rueben up in Milwaukee, when he attempted to give Yvette a little more motivation to find the cop, by popping up on her in traffic.

***

Reuben's eyes went wide when he saw the Ford Expedition that T.G. had been next to peel off and charge at his shooters.

"What the fuck?" he said.

A number of them started shooting at it, but it did not slow down. A few seconds later, it rammed the van that was in the middle after the squad of killers dove out of the way. Up in front of the Escalade, the armed driver and the armed passengers both had jaws dropped nearly in their laps. They then saw the pickup truck that the target was in peel off and follow the Expedition.

***

BOCKA! BOCKA! BOCKA! BOCKA!

T.G. floored it and with his hand hanging out of the window, he fired at any one of the shooters, popping one of them in the face.

Bullets flew like swarms of angry bees as he fled. He stayed low as he got on the lieutenant's tail. Glancing in his rearview mirror, T.G. could see the men jumping back in their vans to give chase.

"Who the fuck are they?" he wondered to himself as he hit 64 miles an hour, passing the abandoned vehicles littered all over the road by their drivers that heard the shooting.

Suddenly, T.G. noticed Michael's SUV swerving. In an attempt to see what the hell the lieutenant was doing, T.G. shot into the left lane and ran up on the driver's side of the Expedition.

He saw the blood splatter on the lieutenant's window. He could just make out the old man's head, jerking around, trying to stay up.

"Shit...shit...shit! Michaels!" T.G. panicked, realizing that the man who was like a father to Yvette and Julie was hit, caught by gunfire meant for him. T.G. frantically beeped his horn, trying to get Michaels' attention, hoping it would get him to come back to and slow to a stop. Then T.G. could rush him to the E.R.

But up ahead was another big intersection, jam packed with traffic.

"Michaels! Aaayyyeee! Waaake uuuup!" T.G. pleaded, laying on the horn, tears filling his eyes as he spotted a city bus, directly ahead of Lieutenant Michaels. He then saw the man's head hit the window and it stayed there, not moving anymore. T.G. let off the gas and started slowing down. The Expedition continued pushing, at speeds of more than seventy miles an hour.

Already cringing, T.G. watched in horror as Lieutenant Michael's Expedition slammed into the rear of the bus so hard, it caused a massive explosion that caught three vehicles sitting next to the bus, instantly frying the people inside. T.G. sat there, stoically watching the fiery wreckage burn. People that had not perished jumped out of their vehicles and ran far away from the fire.

He couldn't believe it. Jarvis Michaels was dead, all because of him. He hadn't been able to take out the man that had taken him, Bucks, Yvette and Julie into his and his wife's home, after Colombians came so close to ending them all, and had saved all four of them from certain death, delivered by Webster in a garage owned by a Colombian kingpin. But Michaels was gone. He was dead, body burning to a crisp, right before his very eyes.

A flash of white caught T.G.'s attention just then. He looked up into the rearview and saw them coming. Two of the vans, but with them, he saw a black Cadillac truck. Teeth clenched, fire in his eyes, T.G. set his handgun down on the center console, reached over to the passenger side floor and got his Plan B out of the duffle bag. Seeing that they were just about ten or fifteen seconds away from reaching him, T.G. wasted no time getting into action. "I am definitely gonna' need a vacation after this," he told himself and opened the door, ready to go to war all by himself.

***

"Come on, come on! Go! Hurry up!" Reuben shouted, holding his Colt CAR-15, fitted with monkey-nuts and altered into a fully automatic spitter. Looking through the open partition divider, Reuben could see out of the windshield. The two vans were side by side, racing to catch up with the target, down a divided highway.

Weaving in and out of the lanes, the driver of the Cadillac truck swerved around the abandoned vehicles in the road. A quarter of a mile up, he saw the pickup's taillights come on. His eyes shifted to the Expedition, and saw that it was not slowing down, but swerving. Seconds later the driver, passengers, and Rueben, witnessed the SUV crash into the back of the bus and cause a massive explosion, that set off a chain reaction of explosions, killing so many people in mere seconds.

"Whoa. Who the hell was in that SUV, man?" Reuben asked aloud.

"It has police license plates, jefe," the man in the passenger's seat said.

"A cop? Aw, yo, please, let it have been that fucking gringo that killed my primo!" Rueben hoped.

"Shit! Boss, look!" the driver panicked.

Reuben looked just in time and saw the pick-up truck speeding backwards. One of the vans swerved out of its path, but the other wasn't lucky enough. The rear end of the Silverado hit the side of the van as the driver attempted to swerve left but made the van slide sideways instead.

The van flipped up into the air, tossing and turning with its load of shooters inside as the pick-up miraculously continued speeding in reverse. The van slammed to the ground. One person was launched out the windshield and smacked the ground so hard that almost every bone in his body was broken.

"Cuidado!" Reuben shouted when he saw the pick-up right in their path.

The driver and passenger had been so preoccupied with the flying van that neither had been watching the road. Reuben grabbed the door handle and hurried to open the door. He hurled himself out of the Escalade as the pick-up and the Escalade collided, killing the driver and passenger instantly.

Tumbling and rolling until he came to a stop, Reuben cursed, face scraped and bleeding from the asphalt. The sound of machine gun fire erupting quickly got his attention. He managed to look up and saw that the target he had thought was in the pick-up had started dumping at the van that had the remaining hitters in it.

They hopped out and looked at the Silverado, going in reverse. They had not known that the man they were sent to kill was not inside, but hiding on the other side of a Toyota Prius, holding a big-ass gun.

***

T.G. fired the automatic .50 caliber machine gun like a seasoned Special Forces guerilla, taking out the foolish shooters with the element of surprise on his side. He was glad the heavy toolbox was in the pick-up when he stole it. It had made the perfect weight to keep the gas pedal floored, and using the seat belt to tie the steering wheel, he slammed it in reverse and took off to hide while the runaway helped even out the odds. Within seconds, the nine hitters that had hopped out of the last van lay out in pools of blood, reduced to piles of guts.

Sirens wailed out when T.G. let off the trigger. From the direction he had come, he saw so many red and blue lights flashing. He hurried and ran to the nearest car, an abandoned Honda Civic. He hopped in, relieved that the engine was on. T.G. slammed it into drive and mashed the gas, getting up out of there before any of the cops could get close.

***

Reuben stood off to the side of the road, ducked in a bunch of trees. He saw the man he had been following dip off in a coupe as cops rushed in to flood the scene.

"You can run, my nigga, but just like I found yo' ass before, I can find you again," Rueben said to himself, then took off running through the woods. He made it to the other side, exiting out at a shopping plaza. Seeing a taxicab parked in an empty area, Reuben ran to it and hopped in back, startling the driver. He demanded the old Indian man get to driving, pulling out a wad of cash as an incentive. The man hurried off, motivated by the money. Reuben pulled his phone out and made a call. It was answered after five rings.

"This better be important, you fucking spic!"

"Bitch! Who the fuck you callin' a spic?" Rueben snapped.

"Oh…it's you…sorry."

"You will be if you ever come out cho' body again!"

"I said sorry, Reuben! What's going on?"

"That bitch ass nigga got away! I need you to track him again for me! Fast!"

"I need ten more grand for that," she told him.

"I got ten bullets."

"I can't spend those."

"I know! Make it happen or I will expose you, then I'ma chop yo' muthafuckin' head off and feed it to the crocodile!"

Reuben ended the call then, heated to the point that his head hurt. He felt eyes on him as he brooded angrily. Looking forward, he caught the cabbie looking at him in the rearview.

"Fuck is you lookin' at, dude?"

The Indian looked forward, refraining from replying with words, out of fear of the dangerous thug in his back seat.

Chapter 9

Bucks stood as still as an antelope that felt the predator coming for it, from some unknown location. He couldn't believe what he just heard. Gunshots, agonized yelling, Michaels telling him that it was a wrap and to bring the girls home, if it was the last thing he ever did. His eyes welled with tears, Bucks heard what sounded like a loud explosion, then the line went dead.

"What the fuck, Joe?" he asked himself.

The part that had Bucks beside himself was Michael's revealing that T.G. had pulled up and was about to dome him, but he hesitated, then the shooters pulled up and pandemonium broke out.

"You good, my nigga?" asked Flip.

Standing next to Bucks in the dirt lot of the makings of a strip mall and arcade/movie theatre complex Bucks had invested just over one point five million dollars of cocaine and dope money in, Buck's right-hand man had been there at the beginning of the call and had heard it all. Bucks wasn't easily rattled. Flip knew something big had gone down.

"Michaels is dead, bro," Bucks told him.

Flip's eyes went wide in shock. "Whaaat? How, nigga?"

"T.G. pulled up on him, finna pop him, but the ol' man said that nigga didn't shoot. He hesitated."

"So…what happened?"

Bucks told Flip what the lieutenant said happened. It had Bucks vexed and puzzled.

"Latinos, though? Why some 'migos, man?"

Bucks pondered about it. He couldn't think of a reason why a gang of Hispanics would get to hopping out and trying to hit T.G., until he remembered the Colombian dude that had come to light them all up at his and T.G.'s spot up in the 'Mil.

"Yvette and JuJu had beef with a Colombian dude when the cop that caught me and T.G. up escaped from there. If I'm right, that nigga is a big dog, bruh."

"Great. Now we at it with crooked cops, bitch ass niggas in our own hood and a dick-head-ass kingpin?" Flip said, making sure he understood the whole situation.

Bucks nodded. "Seems that way, fam."

Flip shook his head. "Guess I need to make a trip to the gun store and ante-up. I refuse to let any of these pussy muthafuckas win, Joe."

Bucks dapped his homie up. He was grateful to have real niggas on his team. The fakes that virtually outnumbered the real, folded up like paper cranes, and couldn't hold up to a gust of wind, let alone to going toe to toe with connected individuals, that were not easy to beat.

"We got a lot of work to do, my nigga. I know who to call to find out if that Columbian nigga's back in town," Bucks said, pulling out his iPhone and calling Javi up.

"Holla," Javi answered.

"I think dude came back to town from Colombia, fam. Shit just went down."

"I'm on it, my nig'. Trust 'n believe," Javi swore, then ended the call.

***

Samantha tapped her stiletto angrily, pissed as shit hat T.G. was not answering his phone. She had called five times, sent life-threatening texts, then hit the button to activate the deadly ankle monitor on his leg. She cursed angrily when she saw the device was no longer on him, but in a deep lake.

Sitting across from her in the large Subway restaurant, Bernice chuckled. Samantha wanted to smack the woman. Glaring at the still very beautiful Polish chick, a dirty blonde with an athletic figure, wearing a dark blue sweater dress with a turtleneck, brown leather stiletto boots, and big gold earrings. Samantha found herself constantly being compared to Berniece and it burned her up.

She herself was in a tight-fitting, white long-sleeved dress with roses all over it, nude-pantyhose, and red heels on her feet. Bernice had natural glamor to her, while Samantha had her nose fixed and had been contemplating getting breast and ass enhancement surgeries. The older she got, the more she wanted to do to herself to stay looking young and attractive.

"Mind telling me what's funny?" Samantha asked her partner in crime, and against crime.

"You and how I can see this all blowing up in your face like I told you it would," Berniece told her. "Your limp dick husband has you doing his dirty work, and you don't even give a shit about him. I am thoroughly puzzled by that, Sammie."

"It's all a part of my plan, nosey bitch. When it's all said and done, I will be the last one standing."

"And your new friend?" Berniece asked, eyeing Samantha curiously. "Not the one that managed to disarm and cut that ankle bracelet off of him."

"He's dangerous, maybe even more dangerous than Tremaine," Samantha said, growing aroused at the thought of the Latino sexing her down rough and wild like T.G. did. "I'm keeping him, for a while at least."

Berniece shook her head. "What would you like on your tombstone, and I don't mean pizza."

Samantha looked at her. "Just wait 'n see. I still have an Ace in my hand, 'Niece, the Ace of spades."

"Maybe you should toss it out then, because it's really looking like you're not gonna' get home, chick."

Samantha chuckled. "Hurry up and finish your sub. We've got places to be, and criminals to see."

***

Webster grinned as he listened to the chatter on the police radio he had. The news of Lieutenant Michael's death had him feeling like he had just bowled a strike.

"Sir?"

He heard the voice of one of his deputies. Turning towards the doorway, he saw the shaggy-faced plain clothes trooper there.

"What is Niles?" Webster asked.

"I just wanted to extend my condolences about Lieutenant Michaels. He was a good man and a great cop, sir."

Webster gave a fake nod. "Thank you, Deputy. I'm a little busy, though. Please close my door."

The deputy nodded and did as he was told. Webster leaned back with a big smile on his face.

"One down, three to go and two probably in east Kambumfuck getting stretched out like the whores they always strived to be. Life couldn't get any better than this."

***

Julie cried her eyes out. The pain was past unbearable, but she couldn't move either of her arms or her legs. She was bound, facing down, to the four-steel post on the dingy bed. On top of her, a heavy man grunting, breath smelling like ass, beer and cigarettes. He pumped himself in and out of her asshole relentlessly, not giving a shit how much he was hurting her. He had paid more than five hundred to fuck the pregnant Asian chick in her ass, and he had absolutely no intentions of not getting his money worth.

Despite the agonizing pain that had filled her with dread and disgust for the last twelve men that had violated her just that day, Julie could only see the horrific betrayal that had gotten her there. And she didn't even know where she was. Wherever she had been taken, the people spoke Spanish. For the past few days of vaginal and anal torture, she still had not seen Yvette. She didn't even know if her best friend/secret lover was alive.

"Please, God! I know I've done some horrible things in my life, but please! Spare us! I wanna have my baby and make it back to Bucks! I want Yvette to find love! Real love! We already lost Rock and Sir! Please don't let us lose each other."

The rapist then grunted loudly in her ear. Seconds later, she felt him cum inside of her ass, making her cringe at the slimy feeling.

"¡Me encanta este gran culo tuyo!" the man said, still laying on top of her. "Voy a volver para mas, china," he added, then ran his slimy tongue along her neck.

Julie instantly caught chills up her spine, dreading the thought that this was likely where she was going to die, without seeing any of her people again, and never getting to see the product that came from her and the man she loved more than life itself.

**

T.G. hurried into his house and closed the door, locking every extra lock it had. He breathed heavily with relief, so glad he made it home.

"Hey?"

He heard her voice as he sank to the floor, eyes closed, giving thanks to the man above. Denise stood a few feet away from him wearing a ruby red skin-tight Adidas bodysuit, with no shoes or socks on, and her dreadlocks pulled back into a ponytail.

"Tremaine? What happened?" she asked, walking towards him.

T.G. looked up at her. She came to a stop, right in front of him.

"Talk to me. Please," Denise said to him.

He took a deep breath, then he exhaled deeply. "I would really like to go now. Are you packed up?"

Denise nodded her head. "Yeah. Where are we goin', though, Tremaine?"

She reached down to grasp his hands. Helping him to his feet, Denise wrapped her arms around him and held him tightly.

"Let's go where Black folks run it," T.G. suggested, with his arms wrapped around her waist, loving how she felt in his arms.

"I guess that means I'll find out when I get there because the only places that Black people run things is down south."

T.G. smiled. For a reply, he leaned down and planted a soft kiss on her forehead. Then he took her by the hand, led her to her room, so he could help her get her and Letoya's things, and get the hell out of Illinois, possibly forever, without the threat of instantaneous death by jellyfish toxin keeping him a slave to Samantha any longer.

***

"We should meet up sooner than later." Bucks sat in his GTO at a red light, reading the response to his questioning the identity of the random texter. They told him a mutual friend, then followed up with the suggestion to meet up soon.

"When you feel the need to say who you are, then maybe I might acknowledge you further. Until then, get up off my jack." Bucks sent the text and was getting ready to pull off, when a shiny black Mercedes screeched to a stop next to him. He went for his pistol, on it, ready to dump on the driver, when the tinted window rolled down. He remembered her face right away.

"Care to acknowledge me now, Bernard?" she asked.

His eyebrows furrowed. "You got some serious balls, poppin' up on me like this," he told her, gripping his cannon so tightly that his hand trembled.

"Been through hell 'n back, sir, nothing rattles me. Follow me, and I will bestow upon you a few very valuable tips," she said.

The light turned green just then. Bucks watched her peel off. He started rolling and found himself following her to an empty parking lot, with a closed-down Burger King. He followed her to the back of the boarded up fast-food joint and parked behind her E63 AMG. The woman got out. Bucks couldn't help but to slightly lust over the woman. He knew she was older, likely in her forties, and she was short, like five-five or five-six. The blue sweater dress she had on clung to her, revealing big breasts, a slim waist, nice hips, and a round ass. She had brown leather boots on that looked like what women that rode horses wore on her feet. She was what Bucks remembered older folks calling women of a certain age that were still gorgeous, a fox. Her dirty-blonde hair added to her devilishly sexy white girl appeal, the type that had men craving to fuck, just to say they did it.

***

"I would love to know why I shouldn't just pop yo' ass right now," Bucks said to her through his open window.

She leaned down, resting her arms on the ledge of the window. Her breasts came within inches of him. Her perfume smelled like candy.

"Because Bernard, if you shoot me, not only will you die, right now…" She paused as a little red dot appeared on his chest. Bucks saw it and felt his heart drop. "But you will not find Sergeant Jones, nor Sergeant Tran. And believe me…they need you."

Bucks looked up into her eyes and saw pure evil in them. He wanted to grab her and choke a booger out of her ass. But her words… She knew where his pregnant fiancée and his home girl were.

"Somethin' tells me that you're gonna send me on a treasure hunt."

She grinned. "If you consider those two gold and diamonds, then yes, I am. But first, you are going to listen to what I have to say, and then you might have an easier time."

"Okay?"

He listened to what she told him. As her information entered his ear, registering his brain, Bucks grew so irate that he could literally feel his temperature rising to the point of exploding.

"It is one seriously fucked up world we live in," she concluded, tapping the door. "I will be in touch. Unlike her, that dirty whore. I will take care of you, so that when you get your woman back, you two can walk the aisle and have no worries."

"And Yvette," Bucks clarified.

"Of course. Can't forget about our dear crazy Jones. Tah-tah, now, sir."

The red dot disappeared from Bucks' chest. He watched the woman get back into her AMG Benz and peel off. He sat there for minutes past her exit, then he let out a loud yell, beyond astounded that he had such a bumpy, broken up road in front of him.

***

Six Hours Later…

The plane touched down a little after eight in the evening. Denise held her baby while she looked out of the first-class window, seeing how busy the Hartsfield-Jackson Atlanta International Airport was. She smiled, feeling a sense of peace. With all the troubles being left hundreds of miles away, back in Illinois, she truly felt a heavy weight lifted off her chest.

Looking over to her left, T.G. was passed clean out. She was surprised that he hadn't felt the big Boeing land, but she knew that he had been through hell in the past few days. Denise leaned over and kissed his cheek. T.G.'s eyes fluttered until they opened. The captain's voice came over the speaker system, announcing that they were in Hot-Lanta, the time zone had changed, to enjoy their stay if they were just visiting and thanked them for flying.

"You okay?" Denise asked T.G., as the plane taxied to the rolling hallway that led into the airport terminal.

T.G. nodded his head. "I actually feel real rested." Once the plane reached its final stop, T.G. got their luggage that they came on with, then followed Denise and her daughter out of the plane.

***

Waiting outside for them was a brand new S580 Mercedes Maybach Benz. The driver, a short woman with skin the color of cinnamon, and dusty brown hair in neat intricate cornrows, wearing a green sleeveless top, a Burberry pencil-skirt, and nude Louboutin pumps stood posted next to the car. The second she saw T.G., she lit up and ran to him, flinging herself into his arms.

Denise felt a twinge of jealousy.

This nigga got too many hoes in his life. I'ma have to step it up, she thought, as the embrace continued for way longer than normal friends did.

Letoya screeched just then. Denise looked down at her little one and saw that she was smiling up at her.

"Aww! She is so cute, gurl!"

Denise turned and saw the girl just inches away from her. She had to admit, the chick was incredibly gorgeous. In a way, to Denise, the girl had an uncanny resemblance to the singer Tinashe.

"How ol' is she?" the girl asked, with a very strong Georgia twang.

Denise glanced at T.G. He stood back nodding his head, as if to let her know that it was okay.

"Two months," she finally told her, "and her name is Letoya."

"So adorable. Hi. My name's Charlise, 'n T.G. is my cuzzin'. He's tol' me a lot about you. Welcome to my city, gurl."

Denise looked at T.G. again. He was smiling now.

"Thank you, Charlise. I never been to Atlanta before, but I've seen lots of it on TV and music videos."

Charlise chuckled. "Oh naw, gurl. We gon' show you how it really goes down in the A, 'ya feel me, kinfolk?"

"Aye, cuz. Remember what I told you," T.G. chimed in, giving Charlise a look.

She nodded. "Right. My fault, 'cuzzo. Well, Denise, maybe when 'thangs cool off a 'lil bit, we can turn up togetha, but fo' this go 'round, it's gon' be you, this beautiful angel, and my cray-cray cuzzin."

"Next time then," Denise agreed, as Charlise began to not seem so bad.

Right at that moment, a vibrantly candy-painted '73 Chevy Impala convertible, sitting high up on twenty-six-inch rims pulled up behind the glossy black Maybach.

"A'right, y'all. Cuz, make 'sho you bring 'nem on by so I can cook y'all a real breakfast."

"Definitely, fam. Who that is in the Chevy though?" T.G. asked, trying to figure out who the dreadhead behind the wheel was, since they didn't get out of the car.

"That's my bae, cuz. He just got out of the feds 'n he's really doing good fo' himself."

"What about for you?" T.G. replied, still eyeing the man, who just sat there looking at him.

"I got me, Tremaine. You know how my daddy raised me, 'cause you know how yo' mama raised you the same way: We take care of ourselves, 'ya dig."

Charlise hugged and kissed him on his cheek, gave Denise a hug, said bye to Letoya, then went and hopped up inside the 'vert. T.G. mugged the dreadhead as he hit the gas and sped by, glancing at him, then looking back out the windshield.

"You must not like him," Denise said.

"A nigga that don't get out the car to open the door for his chick is not who I want my baby cousin fallin' for," T.G. replied., grabbing the bags, and heading towards the Maybach. "And he was lookin' my way like he wanted some smoke. I got plenty for him if he want it."

"No, no, no, Tremaine." T.G. opened up the front door for her. She walked up but paused in front of him. "Positive thoughts. While we're down here, we are gonna' have a good time, enjoy each other's company and no fighting or shooting. Got it?"

He smiled at her. After he nodded his head, Denise smiled back, then cradling her daughter, she got in the car's exclusive diamond quilted leather interior, geeked to be in such a dope-ass ride. T.G. closed her door, put their bags in the trunk, and got behind the wheel.

"She really just let you have her car, thought?" Denise asked as T.G. push-started the twin-turbo V8 engine and put it in drive.

"This is my car, Denise," he informed her, pulling off. "Nobody but Char-Char knows, but I own a luxury car rental agency down here, and it's also a chauffeur car service. She runs it for me.

"Damn. You doin' real good for yourself, T.G. Maybe I can learn a skill and become your employee?"

"Or," he said, with a counter in mind. "You can say fuck bein' a worker and lemme' turn you into a boss."

"A boss, huh? You really think I can be somethin' like that?"

T.G. exited the airport and got en route to the ridiculously pricey hotel he had booked for the three of them.

"You are Black, Denise," he told her. "There isn't a damn thing in the world a Black person can't do or be, if they wanted, and that goes quadruple for Black women, and even Latinas."

"Aww! Tremaine!" Denise gushed over his passion filled words. "I don't know why you're single or why you ain't got no kids, but you keep that shit up, and keep on kissin' me like that, nigga, I'ma cuff yo' ass all the way up."

T.G. busted out laughing at her.

***

Arriving at the luxuriant St. Regis Hotel, T.G. pulled up to the grand main entrance and got out as luggage carriers came with a cart to assist. He went around and helped Denise out with her baby. Their bags went on a cart, and they entered the hotel. Denise was awestruck by the time they got to their exceptional grand suite. She had only seen such greatness on TV. The heels of her six-inch pumps clacked on the shining marble floor as she carried her baby further in.

T.G. couldn't, for the life of him, take his eyes off of Denise's phat bubble booty. The tight ass bodysuit she had on showed her shape off so perfectly, and the stilettos on her feet enhanced it all. She was from the hood, unbelievably gorgeous, a good mother, full of life and along with the aggressive nature she had already revealed to him, she was a very passionate woman with a big phat ass booty.

"This is dope, Tremaine," Denise exclaimed, turning back to him.

"I'm glad you like it. It should suit us for a few weeks, or longer if we need it."

"This can't be cheap," she guessed.

"Don't worry about that. I'm good, so are you, too."

He went and took the bags to the bedroom. She followed behind with the sleeping Letoya in her arms still. Denise gasped at the spacious sleeping section. It was even better than his bedroom.

"Damn...I fucked up," she heard T.G. say just then.

"If this is how you fuck up, then I can't wait to see what it looks like when you don't fuck up."

"Naw...I mean...I fucked up, 'cause there's only one bed."

He dropped the bags on the bed, then looked at her. She had the most comical smile on her face.

"What, you scared to lay in the bed with me or somethin'?" she asked.

T.G. chuckled. "Not in any way shape or form, Denise. I just ain't tryna' lead you on. We fuck 'round, get to touchin' n' shit, then I'ma end up puttin the *woo* on yo' ass, then we'll be stuck in bed for days."

"Ha!" Denise laughed, then gasped at herself. "Damn. My bad, but Denise don't get whipped, boo-boo. I does the whippin', so stop bein 'scured and share the bed with me. We'll be aight. We hungry, too. I want some chicken 'n waffles, and so does my baby."

"Letoya has teeth?"

"Chicken 'n waffles-flavored breast milk, duh!"

T.G. laughed his ass off at her. "On everythang, you wild as hell, Joe. Straight up."

You have no idea, playboy, but soon, you will, Denise thought, as images of his naked body invaded her mind again, making her temperature rise, and her flower bloom.

Chapter 10

Four Days Later...

Bucks tried. He tried so hard, but the tears continually filled his eyes. Filled with dread, just sitting there was unbearable. A good man had died, for no reason at all. Bucks' heart cried as he himself did.

The graveyard was filled with family, friends, and coworkers of Lieutenant Jarvis Michaels. His Puerto Rican wife wailed loudly, crying her eyes out. The mob of Spaulding Latin Kings from Humboldt Park, where Mrs. Jarvis Michaels and her dearly departed husband had lived, were present, all of them wearing black shirts with Michaels' face on the front. The large group of Illinois State troopers, county sheriffs from all over the state, local cops, temporarily focused on sending their comrade and friend off the right way.

Lieutenant Sikes was present. His eyes were red and filled with tears. He had lost a great friend and was seething. Bucks sat next to Michaels' wife, holding her, doing his best to console her. He knew that it would be near impossible for her to smile for quite some time. The two had never had children. She was now alone in her house. Two people approached Bucks. He saw the black pumps with black pantyhose feet first, then looking up, he saw the two women in black dresses that he would give anything at the moment to put a machete to.

Samantha and Bernice stood there looking as if they wanted to laugh but tried to contain it. Bucks envisioned both of their heads exploding.

"Mrs. Michaels. We're sorry for your loss," Samantha said, looking at the Boricua Latin Queen, avoiding Bucks' glare. Sikes approached as Michaels' wife looked up at Samantha. Bucks felt coldness coming from the two women, and the heat that radiated from Sikes.

"Thank you," Mrs. Michaels said with a broken voice. "He was my everything. I can't believe someone would do this to such a good man."

"It's sad," Samantha replied. "There are some truly evil people in this world, ma'am. I'm just said that one of our own lost his life and we failed to protect him."

One day, I'ma slice this bitch's lips off and make her eat them, Bucks thought, as his ears burned from her vile concoction of fabricated emotions.

"Rest assured though, ma'am," chimed in Bernice, touching Mrs. Michaels' shoulder. "We will get everyone that is involved in Lieutenant Michaels' death."

She cast Bucks a quick glance, then she and Samantha looked at Sikes. Mrs. Michaels' eyes went back towards the grass as memories of more than twenty years of marriage flooded her mind. She missed the silent threats being eye-swapped between the women and Sikes.

"See you around...Lieutenant," said Samantha, with obvious sarcasm.

The two left off, leaving behind so many plots of death upon them.

***

Webster smiled as he watched the live camera feed on the iPad in his hands. The burial was filmed by the hidden camera on his wife's sunglasses. He saw the misery in the eyes of Michaels' wife, and fury in Lieutenant Sikes and Bucks' eyes.

"Smiles, guys. Nobody can hurt your punk-ass friend anymore. Now, I will focus on you two," he said to himself.

Samantha and Bernice hopped up into his Ford Explorer just then.

"Great work, ladies," he said to them, with a big smile.

"Up yours, asshole," said Samantha, as she went into her handbag to get her phone out and got ahold of her new boy toy.

"And to think that a funeral is supposed to bring people together," Webster replied, shaking his head as he pulled off.

He glanced at Bernice in the rear-view mirror. She looked at him and gave him a wink, then turned her head to look out of her window, smirking at the things inside of her head that were going to seriously shake things up.

***

Lieutenant Sikes brooded long and hard. What Bucks had just told him about Samantha's roadie had him perturbed.

"Those two bitches have some serious issues," Sikes said.

"I really cannot understand how all of this happened in the first place, man. I was just a young nigga gettin' bucks wit' my bro. Now, my homie is my number-one enemy, my wife and her homegirl are God knows where in danger, cops are at me, I'm ridin' wit' cops... this shit is crazy, Joe."

Sikes nodded in understanding. He knew the predicament was tough for Bucks. He had no intentions of letting the young gunner go at any of the drama alone.

"Bernard. Listen to me," Sikes said to him.

Bucks listened closely as the man ran down a long list of plans to combat all the bullshit clouding life at the moment. The more Bucks heard, the angrier he became, but also, he became more confident. He then realized that the straight and narrow lieutenant was not so straight and narrow.

"Trust me," Sikes said, wrapping it all up. "This will work. Play your part, and this will all pan out."

Bucks nodded his head, then turning away he went back to Mrs. Michaels, to rejoin her and the huge crowd of people, surrounding her with love and condolences.

***

T.G. walked alongside Denise in the peaceful Atlanta Botanical Garden, enjoying the scenery and the fresh smells of so many kinds of foliage. For the past four days, they had been shopping, gone to a few restaurants, and to the movies. Denise had gotten a stroller for her daughter, a crib built by T.G. in their grand suite's bedroom and had been learning the ropes in many of T.G. 's southern ventures. The respect and admiration she had already developed for him had increased ten-fold. Discovering that he had not only the foreign auto rental and car service, but had a couple of rim shops, paint shops, and tattoo parlors. She saw that he had a vast portfolio of hustles, not to mention the dope he had being moved around by a mob of Charlise's people out in Bankhead, up in East Atlanta, and even down in Macon.

She respected his hustle, and was enamored by his swag. He was still so mysterious to her, and it had her swooning over him. Her daughter even took a major liking to him. Whenever he held her, Letoya smiled and giggled. Denise felt herself falling for him, but what had her puzzled was that T.G. had not made a move on her, besides for a kiss here and there.

Dressed to impress and to stay cool in the still very hot weather, Denise had on a white Gucci tank top shirt, a red Gucci snake-skin skirt with a slit up the front and white Gucci sling-back pumps on her feet, emphasizing freshly, waxed and oiled legs. T.G. pined over her, the gorgeous dreadhead as they hopped into the Maybach and headed off, and yet Denise found herself wondering why his hands had not been all over her. She was digging on him hard, especially in his Balenciaga fit, with the sneakers that went with it, and his diamond jewelry.

She herself had some new drip around her neck, in her ears, on wrist, and on a few of her fingers. Nearly ten grand worth of drip had Denise sparkling, but she wanted him on her, heating her up, instead of his ice making her freeze.

***

"Tremaine? I have a question," she told him, when they stopped to sit at a table in a section for those in need of a break.

"Lay it on me," he told her, sitting across from her and her baby.

"Um...I..." Denise stopped and sighed to herself. She found it hard to verbalize what she was thinking.

"What's wrong? You okay?" he asked, seeing the bothered look on her face.

She shrugged. "I guess.... I'm just curious about you, is all. I know you're attracted to me, but..."

T.G. smiled. He knew what was on her mind.

"Listen to me, Denise." He scooted forward and took her hands into his. "I told you when you asked why I spared you...I have done a lot of fucked up things, and I have wronged people, people that I care about. It eats at my soul every day. I am very into you, but if it's in the cards for us, I gotta make sure that I do right by you... 'cause it isn't just you. Letoya deserves a good father, biological or not, and you deserve a king."

Denise could feel her heart beating fast as the rich gangster sitting across from her spit words full of passion and sincerity. She wanted so badly to jump on him and kiss him all over. Never before had she had a man like him falling for her.

"You are a king, T.G. For the fact that you can admit wrong doings, and how I can actually see remorse in your eyes, I know you are for Letoya and me."

T.G. smiled at her. "You hungry?"

She nodded her head.

"Aight. Lemme' go hit the head and we'll shoot to this lil spot I Googled," he told her, then he got up and headed to the men's restroom.

Denise's heart swelled in her chest as she watched him walk away. She sighed, wondering if love really could be had at first sight. As she floated off into so many visions of what could be, her thoughts were interrupted when a woman with golden-blonde dreadlocks, wearing a black t-shirt that had a duffle bag overflowing with cash on the chest, skintight skinny leg jeans with cuts on them, and spiked toed Red Bottom stilettos.

"Hello, Denise. Nice to finally meet you," the caramel skinned girl said to her.

"Uh…. who are you?" Denise asked, her hands going towards her handbag where her ceramic flip-knife was stashed.

"No need for names at the moment, and I wouldn't attempt to pull out any weapon. You won't make it out of that seat if you do," the woman declared. "Have no worries, not now. I'm here to keep you and Letoya company while my husband has a little talk with Tremaine."

***

T.G. groaned as he drained his bladder. Closing his eyes, he leaned his head back. He had been hesitant to leave Denise and Letoya's side, but he had to take a piss so bad.

"Damn that felt good," he said to himself, shaking his joint then tucking himself in.

He flushed, turned around, and found a tall, muscular light-skinned man with long braids standing in the middle of the bathroom, with two pistols in his hand and a mean mug on his face.

T.G.'s heart dropped.

"What up, homeboy," the man said to him. "You and I are gonna' have a chat, if you lie, you will die. Period. Got it?"

Having no choice, T.G. nodded his head.

"Good. Wash yo' hands first. I ain't talkin' to a nigga that just took a leak and hasn't washed his hands."

***

Samantha's eyes went wide when he grabbed her by her fragile throat and slammed her up against the wall. He dwarfed her by almost a foot, and he was very strong, and he was very angry. She had gone to meet him. At the little motel, out on the edge of unincorporated Zion at the busily travelled Highway Route 41 and Route 173, Samantha had been about to knock on the door when it suddenly opened up, and she was yanked inside by the man himself.

She shrieked in fear as he muscled her up against the wall.

"I should fucking kill you for playin with me, perra!" he told her through clenched teeth.

"I…I'm…not!" Samantha managed to say, though he was cutting her air off. "I swear!"

"Then why don't I know where that bitch ass nigga is yet?"

"R-Rueben! Let m-me go! P-Please!"

She felt his grip loosen up a second later. He lowered her to her heels but kept her pressed against the wall. Samantha looked up at the braided-up Columbian. He damn near literally scared the shit out of her, but he also excited her. The way he had damn near killed her, with one hand, had her wondering how aggressive he was when it came to the other things.

"If I don't have his location in twenty-four hours, I won't stop until you stop breathing forever!" he growled. "Yo' ass a fed! Act like it and find that bitch ass nigga!"

"Okay!" Samantha shouted. "Stop yelling at me, dammit! I didn't come here for that shit!"

"Then what the fuck you come here for, bitch?" Rueben demanded, ready to strangle Samantha.

"I came for this!" She reached out and grabbed his crotch, squeezing his cock through his Amiri jeans. "All of this!" she added, refusing to let it go. "I've wanted it since I first laid eyes on you, Reuben! Give it to me!"

Reuben's frown morphed into a smirk. "Oh, so you want you some rich-nigga dick, huh, bitch?"

"Yes! I want rich nigga dick!" Samantha told him.

Rueben open hand smacked Samantha across her face. *Whop!* Her head snapped to the right. Her nipples got hard, and her pussy got wetter. She turned her head and looked back at him. "That all you got, you fuckin nitwit?"

Rueben grabbed her and threw her halfway across the room. She landed on the bed and bounced on it. Before she could even sit up, Rueben was on her. He forced her dress up over her hips, pushed her legs open, then he ripped the crotch of her pantyhose open, exposing that she wasn't wearing any panties.

Samantha leaked with anticipation. She had been dreaming of the cocaine drug lord giving her the dick, hard and rough like she was just a dirty little whore. Rueben dropped his pants, revealing eight hard inches of circumcised Colombian dick, throbbing like it had a heartbeat of its own. She saw it and almost exploded from the sight. When he jumped on the bed, Rueben muscled her over, onto her stomach, then pulled her ass up into the air. He smacked her ass hard. He ripped her pantyhose even more, then he gripped her ass cheeks, opening them up to expose her puckered asshole. Rueben spit a wad of saliva down into her crack, getting her booty hole wet. Samantha prepared for him once she felt him slathering it all over her pinkness. She felt the tip enter her and stretch her out. The pain it came with had her squealing, grabbing, and squeezing the bed sheets while her toes curled up in her shiny red pumps.

"Yeah, bitch! This what you wanted, puta? Huh?" Rueben growled through clenched teeth, as he pumped in and out of the woman's tight asshole.

"Yeeeesss! Oh, God, yeeess, it is, Rueben! Oh, my God, it feels so good!" Samantha cried out.

Rueben got rougher. He smacked her ass repeatedly, pulled her hair, fucked her like she was a Hollywood whore. She climaxed out of her ass nearly eight minutes later. Her anal tract clenched around his dick, adding heat to his thrusts. His nuts started tingling and the muscles in his back got tight. Feeling his nut rising, Rueben pulled his cock out of her asshole and demanded she turn over.

Samantha obeyed. On her back, she let him climb up onto her chest, then she let him jerk his dick and cum all over her face. She opened her mouth and caught as much of his hot globs as she could.

"Wooooo yeeaah, hoe! You like how this dulce de leche taste?"

"Mmm-hmmm!" Samantha nodded, swallowing a mouthful.

"Good. Yo'bitch ass go be swallowin' all my kids 'erytime I put this dick up in y' white ass," Rueben told her, getting off of her. "Now go do what I told you to do and find that bitch, or the next time I put somethin' up yo' ass, it won't be my dick!"

Samantha got up from the bed. She looked at Rueben once more, then without saying a word, she left the motel room with murder on her mind.

Chapter 11

Bucks cruised west on Buckley Road for the Great Lakes area of North Chicago, in his glossy pearl black Mercedes S63 AMG two-door coupe. Pop Smoke's "Welcome to The Party" bumped. Bucks used the song to get in beast mode. Shit was about to go down, and he could not afford any mistakes.

The music turned down. He blinked, coming out of his head. He glanced over at her and furrowed his eyebrows.

"I love rap, but that guy's voice is annoying," Bernice said.

Bucks shook his head, then he turned the song to Bone Thugs-N-Harmony's "Thuggish Ruggish Bone." With a smirk he glanced over at the dolled-up agent riding next to him. Dressed in a suede, money-green long-sleeved dress, with a gold zipper in the center of it, and a mid-thigh length hem, allowing sexy legs that flowed down to the gold pointed-toe pumps on her feet to show, Bernice was looking real good to Bucks. He hated her but wanted to fuck her, so badly!

Stay focused, nigga! You got the baddest chick in the world! And she's carryin' yo' child! Fuck this hoe-bitch! Handle yo' biz so you can get JuJu and Yvette back! Bucks mentally told himself.

***

Twenty-odd minutes later, Bucks turned right into the driveway at a small building by the border of Libertyville and Grayslake. It had plenty of tall parking lot light poles around the property, but none of them were lit up. Bucks lowered the music and crept towards the rear, which was hidden from the main road that ran past it.

Parked there was a new blacked-out Yenko edition of a Z71 Chevy Silverado, sitting high up via lift-kit, and off-road wheels, and a dark orange Maserati, Gran Turismo Sport convertible. Two women, one wearing a skirt suit, the other in a pants suit stood in front of the Italian-made drop-top. Next to them, a man in black camo gear, looking as big as the body-building version of Arnold Schwarzenegger.

"Who are these people?" Bucks asked Bernice as he pulled up, stopping ten-feet away from them, cutting off his headlights.

He looked over at the foxy agent and saw that she was looking at him.

"They are the people that took your fiancée to where she is, Bernard."

"What?"

Bucks went for his gun but was halted when Bernice grabbed his arm.

"You might not want to do that," she told him.

Red lights entered the car through the windshield. Bucks turned his head and saw the three people now had machine guns in their hands, pointing red beams right at him.

"Use your head. They are here to help you, but if you even think about harming one hair on my head, they will help me. Got it?"

Bucks grinded his teeth. He glared at her with hatred in his eyes.

"Get off of me," he growled.

Bernice smiled at him. "You are one sexy man when you are in gangster mode, Bernard. Maybe when you make it back, you and I can have a little fun.

His eyebrows furrowed at her words. "Make it back?" he questioned.

TAP! TAP! TAP!

He heard tapping on his window. The second he turned his head to the left, and saw one of the women there, pointing her gun at his face. Bernice whipped out a syringe from her handbag and jammed it into Buck's neck. Before he could even begin to put up a fight, she injected him with a sedative that was so strong, that in mere seconds he started becoming weaker and weaker, vision blurring until everything went completely black...

***

Denise sighed as she looked down into the crib. Her daughter was sleeping peacefully with her stuffed Minnie Mouse, and a few more toys that T.G. had bought her. Smiling at memories of the past few days they had been together, Denise wished that they could just stay and build a life as one, in the Black Mecca.

Then the face of the woman with auburn dreadlocks and the Fendi fit flooded her mind. Remembering how the woman never revealed her name, and made her stay put until T.G. returned then left without a world more, had Denise worried sick. The look of forlorn on T.G.'s face only added to her grief, and he wouldn't tell her what was going on. She kissed two of her fingers and placed them upon her daughter's forehead. Turning, Denise left her sleeping infant to go find T.G.

***

She found him out on the balcony. Seeing T.G. through the wide-open glass retracting door to the outdoor lounging space, leaned over the safety rail, looking out over the city of Atlanta, Denise mustered up the courage to go see him, and to make him acknowledge her...all the way.

Denise went up behind him. She wrapped her arms around him, leaning her head against his back. T.G. stayed still for a minute. She could feel him getting more relaxed, his tenseness fading from her touch.

"You aight?" she heard him ask.

She lifted her head up and made him turn to face her. Putting her arms back around him, she looked up at him.

"Are you?" Denise countered.

T.G. gazed down into her eyes. "I wasn't, until ten seconds ago."

"What happened ten seconds ago?" Denise asked.

He wrapped his arms around her then.

"You came to me."

Denise lips parted as his words both shocked and excited her. She was damn near rendered speechless. He had her. She knew it, and she wanted him to know it.

She reached up and pulled him down to her. She pressed her lips to his. She kissed him deeply, passionately. He kissed her back, slowly heating her body up. Their tongues met and danced like there was a love ballad playing. Denise's breathing grew labored as her temperature continued to rise. T.G.'s hands slid down to her hips, then around to cup her juicy ass cheeks. He French-kissed Denise's breath away as he squeezed her meaty buns. His dick grew so hard, pulsating in his boxer briefs as he yearned to be inside of her. He could still smell traces of her perfume, and it was driving him insane!

Denise felt one of his hands leave her ass. Seconds later, she felt it going up the front of her skirt, then the feeling of a lone finger tracing her wetness through the thin fabric of her wet lace thong made her feel like T.G. had taken a blow torch to her. She moaned as his fingers pressed a little harder. She opened her legs, lifting her right leg up, inviting him to do more.

T.G. stopped kissing her suddenly. Baffled, Denise looked at him, ready to declare war on him for stopping.

"I don't wanna' hurt you, Denise," he told her, as thoughts of all that he had done that had affected his entire world, and the woman he still very much loved.

"You won't, T.G. I'm ready, baby. I want you so bad. I know you can tell," she told him, as she leaked even more to the point that her pussy was dripping down her thighs. He could. She was so wet and hot for him. Her lips were swollen from his kiss, and her heart was beating for him. T.G. pulled his hand from under her skirt. He put his wet fingers to his lips, then sucked her juices from them. Denise bit her bottom lip, turned on to the max by him tasting her. He grabbed her, picked her up by her ass, hoisting her up. Denise wrapped her legs around him. He carried her over to the lounge couch by the exterior wall of the deck and sat her down.

T.G. took a step back and one piece at a time, stripped naked for her, until it was him, his muscles, tattoos, and ten inches of hard dick dying to get wet from a dip in her hot tub. Denise licked her lips at the sight of him. At the sight of it. She had pictured T.G. being hung, but he was packing way more than she thought.

He stepped to her, pulled her up. She couldn't resist wrapping her hand around his length. She felt how warm and smooth he was, how thick and how very likely it was what she craved to give her that. Ultimately, T.G. made her release him, so he could undress her. He lifted her tank top off, then unsnapped her lace bra, freeing her perky breasts. Her nipples were erect and aching for his mouth on them.

He unzipped her shirt and pulled it down to her ankles, then he pulled her thong down. Denise stepped out of them and stood before him with sexy white Gucci sling-backs on, bare right along with him, like a Black Adam and Eve. She ran her hands over T.G.s toned six-pack abs, biting her bottom lip, turned on by his physique. She was loving the incredible specimen of pure man that was in front of her.

Denise took his hardness back in her hand, gripping his wood like she never wanted to let it go.

T.G. was ready to sit her back down and dive in headfirst, to take a trip to peach cobbler town and taste the sweet goodness gracious he knew was yearning for him. But she had her own ideas and refused to let him do all the pleasing and teasing. Ladies first, she told herself. She gazed up into his eyes, already picturing him trying to run from her mouth game.

She slowly fell down to her knees, before him, kneeling like a submissive queen to her dominant king. Her pussy continued to leak with anticipation of what came after the foreplay. Holding him at the base, Denise opened her mouth, stuck her tongue out and licked from the bulbous tip, down his shaft to his balls. She made circles around his nut sack. T.G. shuddered, toes wiggling, then curling up.

"Shit!" he cursed, when Denise sucked his nuts into her mouth, and began pleasuring them while she jerked his cock with her right hand. She teased him, aiming to make his head explode like she wanted him to do. She massaged his balls with her mouth, making T.G. go crazy. He threw his head back when she released his balls and took his cock into her warm mouth. He groaned, feeling her deep throating him. He put his left hand to the back of her head, and started gently fucking her mouth, feeling his dick slide down her throat.

Denise reached under him and cupped his balls. She cradled them, massaging them while orally pleasing him. T.G. cursed and groaned, mind blown by it all. He wanted to keep going and bust his nut in her mouth but remembering what he had been tasked to do by the armed thug in the bathroom, T.G. wanted to make her remember him because there was no guarantee that he was coming back.

He took his dick from her, pulled her up from her knees, laying her down on the couch. He took control of her, pushing her legs out wide, opening her all the way up, so he could go all the way in, headfirst. Denise moaned, hissing pleasurably as he kissed and licked all over her. He kissed her left nipple, then gently sucked on it, swirling his tongue around it, while he massaged the other.

"Tremaine! Oooo, baby! Shid!" she cursed.

He switched, sucking her right breast, massaging her left. Denise was on fire, burning up as if she was walking through the blazes that had destroyed Paradise. He made his way down to her stomach, kissing his way down to her swollen center. Face to face with her flower, T.G. smelled her, taking her scent in. His mouth watered like he was sucking on a piece of sweet and sour candy.

Denise felt him part her swollen lips. His lips met them and kissed them. She squirmed, her belly twitched and her nipples got even harder. She grasped her breast, arched her back so that her pussy was in his face even more. T.G. found her clit and took it into his mouth. Denise cried out the second he began sucking on it. She felt like the bones in her body were no longer there, like she had just become putty. She panted, breathing heavily as T.G. dined on her like she was a plate of chicken 'n waffles from Roscoe's.

His lips and tongue worked her over so good. She felt like at any minute, she would spontaneously combust and ignite into a ball of flames. She squeezed her breasts hard, attempting to add more sensation to blunt out the mind-blowing bliss he was killing her softly with.

She started thrashing seconds later, grinding her pussy in his face, trying to fuck his mouth. He met her aggressiveness and grabbed her thighs, wrapping his arms up and around them, then burned his face deep in her abyss. Two minutes later, Denise started trembling, convulsing like she was having an exorcism performed on her. She cried out at the top of her lungs, then five seconds later she exploded so hard in his face that it looked like he had gotten hit in the face with a water balloon.

"Whoa! Oh, my God, that was so fucking good!" she exclaimed, as her heart pounded in her chest, the same way her clit throbbed.

T.G. pulled himself from between her legs. He climbed on top of her and looked down into her eyes. "You liked that, baby?" he asked her, in a deep husky tone that gave her goose bumps.

"I did, Tremaine. You bogus as hell, nigga!"

He laughed at her. "How am I bogus, Denise?"

"Because, dammit! You tryna' make a bitch fall in love wit' cho' ass 'n you keepin' secrets 'n shit!"

T.G. smiled at her. He didn't want the mood ruined by the thoughts of having to leave her and Letoya.

"You fallin' in love wit' a nigga already, though?" he asked with a goofy grin that made her cheese up.

"No, nigga! What I look like fallin' in love with a guy that hasn't even gave me the dick yet?"

"Oh. That's the decidin' factor?"

T.G. nestled himself between her legs. The tip of his length rubbed her soaking wet opening. Denise gasped as she felt him easing into her, slowly filling her up.

"You okay?" he asked, pausing to make sure that he wasn't hurting her.

She hissed, "Yeeesssss! Keep goooing, baby!"

T.G. slipped up inside of her and made her moan his name. His eyes rolled to the back of his head, as her tight, warm, and super wet tunnel gripped him like a fitted glove. He groaned from how good she felt. Denise opened her legs wider as T.G. slow-stroked her. He took her hands, weaving his fingers into his, and made love to her. He needed her to remember him. Good love did that, for both women and men.

They went at it for nearly an hour. Him on top of her, her on top of him, he loved her from the side with her leg up in the air, stretching her out like he was a coach, and she was a gymnast. He got her on her hands and knees, made her toot her chocolate ass up in the air. He smacked on it and spread her cheeks open. Aiming to make her go bananas, T.G. lowered his face down into her crack, and kissed her puckered browneye. Denise squealed in the bed sheet when she felt his tongue making circles around it. Her toes curled in her slingbacks, hands down clenching the sheet. She endured the spine-tingling and stimulation for the few minutes, that he gave to her, then she felt him enter her wet-wet from behind.

T.G. went savage on her. He held onto her hips, drilling her so hard and fast that it sounded like there was someone in the room clapping their performance. She called out his name multiple times. Her climax came minutes later. She exploded all over his dick and thighs. T.G. kept going strong until he reached his nut. He couldn't bring himself to pull out of her. It was too good for that. He came so hard that it nearly crippled him. Denise had no complaints at all that he had just come inside of her. Little did he know, T.G. had put more than cum in her in the last hour.

Plopping down next to Denise, T.G. lay on his side breathing hard, muscles bulging, body sweaty. Denise turned to him and scooted in close, feeling so satisfied, safe and cared for. She could still feel her heart beating like a drum. Not once had a man ever so quickly captured her heart like T.G. had just done. Her feelings for him were so overwhelmingly strong that she found herself unable to contain her emotions any longer.

Denise began to cry.

T.G. put his arms around her and held her tightly. No words needed to be said. She was a woman, and he was a man.

"I'm here, Denise. I'm here," he told her.

"For how long, Tremaine?" she asked, knowing that deep in her heart, something was going to take him away from her and Letoya.

He didn't want to tell her the truth. So, he lied.

"For as long as you need me," he capped, then he told her to close her eyes and get some sleep.

Somehow, Denise managed to do so. Within minutes, she was fast asleep, lightly snoring. T.G. waited until he was absolutely sure that she was comatose, before easing himself away from her. When he was off the bed and on his feet, he got to it, finalizing his plans to make sure that no matter what, Denise and Letoya were set …for life.

***

Half an hour later, T.G. had put everything together. Charlise had begged and pleased for him not to go, even threatening to come over and tie him up until he regained some sense. When he called her and told her what he needed for Denise and her daughter, Charlise was all too happy to get it all together. She had grown to really like Denise, and she already loved Letoya. But when she realized that her big cousin was about to go on a mission that he wasn't keeping hope alive on coming back from, Charlise lost it. T.G. had to end the call before she went apeshit on him.

***

He kissed Denise on her forehead, taking a second to appreciate such a beautiful and motivated woman, then made sure that Letoya was still sleep. She was, peacefully, with her Mini Mouse in her arms. He kissed his two fingers, pressed them to the tiny little one's cheek, then T.G. made his way out of the bedroom.

"You took long enough."

T.G. nearly jumped out of his skin when he heard the voice when he exited the bedroom.

He saw the guy that had cornered him in the Botanical Garden's men's room with the twin pistols in his hands, standing next to the chick with the gold dreadlocks.

"How the hell you get in my spot, nigga?"

The guy chucked. "I make things happen, my dude. No more questions. We got a flight to catch."

"To the jungle, right?" T.G. questioned.

"I could have sworn my man said no more questions, nigga!" the beautiful dread head snapped.

The guy chuckled. "My lady isn't nice when clowns piss her off, my man. Now let's go. You have only one chance to make your betrayal right, or somethin' really bad is gonna happen to ya."

T.G. nodded. Without further question, he followed the man out of the suite, with the dread head chick right behind him. He had no clue where he was going, but wherever it was that he ended up, he knew what he had to do, and refused to fail before he took his last breath.

Chapter 12

He couldn't see a thing as he came to, but he could feel a warm wet mouth, swallowing his dick. His arms were stretched up over his head, wrist bound as well as his ankles. He was lying on his back and could tell he had no clothes on. The sound of Spanish music filled his ears. He was all confused.

He heard giggling to the side of him, right after he attempted to pull his arms free. Then the voice of a woman came to his left ear.

"Papi, relajate. Estas en buenas manos con nosotras," he heard but had no clue of what was just said. The blindfold was taken off. Bucks saw all sorts of cosmic colors filling the room he was in. It looked like a private room in a club. Leather couches, a bar, a small stage with a stripper pole under dimmed red light.

Bucks saw two beautiful women, both ass naked, dancing on the stage to the sound of the song. They were getting very X-rated with each other. The space was so dope that momentarily, Bucks hadn't remembered the warm wet feeling engulfing his cock, until he heard moaning down below.

He looked down and saw a cotton-candy pink head of hair bobbing up and down over his cock. The woman paused, released his dick from her mouth then looked at him with such beauty. She smiled, winked, then got back to it, sucking the shit out of his dick. His toes curled with pleasure. A hand cupped his chin and turned his head to the left. Another beautiful Latina was at his side, with red hair, red lipstick, star shaped pasties covering the nipples of her bare breasts. She was tatted up like she wanted to be in the tattoo edition of *Buttz Magazine*. Bucks' eyes went wide as he drank in the bronze chick. She smiled at him. Then she moved in and planted a kiss on his lips.

"Hola, guapo. Bienvenidos a Bogota," she then told him.

What the fuck? Did she just say Bogota? As in Columbia? Bucks thought.

Sure enough, his eyes caught sight of a Colombian flag painted on a wall, with two dancers with phat asses posing in front of it.

"Puta, el no habla español," the chick that had gave him head said to the redhead.

The redhead sucked her teeth. "¡Lo se, cabrñna!" Callate la boca! Solo estoy jodiendo con él."

Bucks was lost. He halfway was thinking that they were talking about what body part they were going to cut off with their machetes. Then the redhead spoke again, this time in English and Spanish.

"You are muy sexy, papi. Desearía que te quieras conmigo para hacer el delicioso toda la noche, pero, we no can. We have to go."

"Go? Hold up! Go where? Why am I in fuckin' Columbia? How the fuck did I get here? And why am I tied up?"

"Ay, Dios Mio, guapo tranquilo!" the other girl said, getting aroused by the thuggish Black man's anger. "We had to welcome you to Columbia in the right way, papi. I no can think of a better manera que waking up to a beautiful naked Columbiana sucking your dick. Can you?"

"Uh…no…I'm engaged. My fiancée would kill me…and you," Bucks told her.

"Hmmmm…maybe we keep secret? Just this once?" she asked.

"Might be best," Bucks agreed.

"Muy bien. My name is Viola, y mi parcera aqui con pelo roja is Paola. We own este lugar that you are in. Paola, unstrap him."

Bucks' restraints were undone. The ladies helped him up and held him steady, while the last of the sedative wore off.

"Ay, Dios Mio. Esa perra es una loca," Paola said, shaking her head. "I no like Bernice at all."

Bucks' eyes went wide when he heard the redhead say Bernice's name.

"You know her?" he asked.

"Si, conocemos a esa perra sucia," Viola said, nodding her head. "She helped us out of drug trafficking charges in your country, pero, she is a bitch."

"Y tambien, her fucking whore friend," Paola added, sneering at the thought of Samantha. "She called us and told us she was sending you here, for us to help you find your mujer. We owe her, so we will help you," she added, as Viola went to the table with bottle of alcohol on it.

There was a flat box and what he could tell was a shoe box on it. Viola brought them to him. Paola helped him to the couch, doing her best to ignore how big his dick was and how badly she wanted to fuck him. Bucks discovered a denim bandana-print Amiri jean and jacket fit, fresh Tom Ford boxer briefs, tank top, socks, in the shoe box was a pair of high-top Amiri bone sneakers, two white gold diamond chains, with a vintage white gold Rolex.

"What the hell?" He looked at the two ladies, puzzled beyond belief.

"Bogota is beautiful, papi. Muy hermosa esta ciudad, pero, can be 'bery ugly," Paola told him, with a serious look on her face.

"La verdad, papi. You have to be careful here, asi que, we have told a few of our people, que a music promoter is coming to find Columbian talent. That is you."

"Wait…what?"

"Ay, Dios Mio," Paola said, shaking her head. "This would be muy easier si hablas espanol."

***

Four Hours Later...
"Oh, shit! Wait, hold up, fam!" T.G. shouted in fear.

Nope! Fuck you, nigga! Get out!" Eric demanded, then he kicked the chair that T.G. was strapped to out of the private jet's open side door.

"Bye-bye, dickhead!" his wife Bunz shouted as T.G. flew out of the Gulfstream, screaming in panic from falling at speeds of over a hundred miles an hour, steadily increasing by the second.

The earth which T.G. saw under him was coming at him fast. His stomach felt like it wasn't even there. He cried his eyes out, terrified, wishing they had just put a bullet in his head, instead of pushing him out of a plane that was tens of thousands of feet above the ground.

He closed his eyes, praying to the Man above to forgive him his sins, when just then, T.G. heard a loud pop. Right after, he was jerked back upwards as if someone had hooked him like a fish and was reeling him in. Opening his eyes, T.G. looked up and saw a parachute had shot up out of the seat, saving him from falling to his death.

T.G. cheered out loud, triumphantly shouting "Yes!" over and over again. He reached the heavily wooded area minutes later, landing softly. Unstrapping himself, T.G. went to get up, when he heard the sounds of footsteps. He looked to his left and gasped in shock when he saw nine familiar faces that he swore had to be figments of his imagination.

"Oye, mal parido!" he heard at his right.

T.G. quickly averted his eyes off of the king of the Valdez family, and his younger cousins, turning his head to the right. He saw the piercing Arctic blue eyes of the Amazon-tall,

New York born Colomborriquena queen of the Valdez family, then he saw her first, then he saw darkness...

***

The large crowd outside of LaVida Noche was deep as hell. Ladies all scantily clad in the naughtiest outfits, with sexy stilettos on, hair done up, faces made up, were looking like they were there to audition for a Maluma music video. Likely because the popular Colombian-playboy singer was set to make an appearance there and turn everyone up. Word of an appearance by Karol G and J Balvin also had so many people ready to go bananas. Bogota was out, ready to party.

The massive hordes of women and men all saw the decked-out convoy of Mercedes trucks, Bentley trucks, Rolls Royce trucks, and so many exotic vehicles pull up, looking as if a dealership had brought its entire inventory out to be showcased.

"El esta aqui! Maluumaaa!" women screamed, then a large number of them started flashing their breasts, while others started twerking. When they saw the owners of the well-known Bogota sex club hop out of the special-order, long-wheel base model Range Rover Supercharged, the guys went wild. Paola Ortiz and Viola Castaneda wore matching Chanel outfits consisting of tiny white tops that tied at their breasts, micro mini flared skirts that let their juicy apple bottom asses show, and they both rocked ankle strapped stiletto pumps, with diamond jewelry, their hair done up intricately, and their makeup on point.

The women in the crowd saw the tall, light-skinned man get out of the Range Rover behind them. They saw his designer fit, his sparkling chains, and some could spot a Rolex mile away. Whistle and catcalls went to him. He looked their way and got winks and smiles and kisses at him. The ladies all figured that he had to be a baller, due to his swag and jewelry, and since he was with Paola and Viola, they surmised that he had to be a sex god.

***

Goddamn! *These hoes out here look like rap video models, Joe*! Bucks thought, seeing all the ladies outside the big club, waiting to get in, while nearly all the guys were picking and choosing which one they were going to get at for the night.

"Vente, papi," Paola said, looping her arm through his. "Remember why we are here."

"Si, papi." Viola looped her arm through his other one, while looking around the crowd with cautious eyes. "A 'bery bad man runs este place. You need to stay focused."

Bucks rolled towards the entrance door with the two ladies at his sides. From the outside looking in, he knew people thought he was a big dog of some sort, but from the inside looking out, Bucks was a ball of nerves. He was in Columbia, by himself, sent there in the most fucked up way, then awakened with his dick in a beautiful woman's life, all because of his quest to find his pregnant fiancée. Guessing at the obvious, Julie was in Bogota. Likely in the club, belonging to this very bad man, who could be just a rich gangster…or the new Pablo Escobar.

The big bouncers at the doors nodded their heads at Paola and Viola as they brought Bucks to the entrance. One man stepped up and looked at Paola.

"Este hombre, ¿quién es?" he asked her.

"Es un promotor de música urbana. Viola y yo query enseñarle como lo hablamos en Bogotá papi. Me entiendes?"

"Tengo que chequear a este hombre," he told her then.

Bucks' heart raced like a Hennessey edition Hellcat in his chest, wondering what the hell they were saying. He had no clue that the bouncer asked Paola who he was, and that she told him that Bucks was an urban music promoter, and that she and Viola just wanted to show Bucks how they did it big in Bogota.

"He needs to pat you down, papi," Paola told Bucks.

Bucks nodded. He wasn't strapped, the ladies told him there was no way anyone that was not from Bogota was getting in with anything but money in their pockets.

The bouncer patted Bucks down then okayed him. The other bouncers stepped aside, while one opened the door to the club. Loud Spanish rap music flowed right out of the club when the door opened up. Paola and Viola took Bucks' arms again and led him inside to what was essentially a giant warehouse with liquor and women all over the place. Blue and purple neon lights flickered on and off. One of Karol G's older songs, with a Puerto Rican/Dominican super star Nicky Jam blared. Ladies danced provocatively on poles on the dance floor, and a few on long ropes that hung from the high ceiling. Bucks was amazed when Paola and Viola brought him into the main area. Then he wondered to himself if he was about to see his pregnant future wife dancing for some creep.

"Where is she?" Bucks asked Viola in her ear. Viola took a deep breath before replying. She knew giving it raw was best but she didn't know him that well, and if he popped off out of instinct, she and Paola were at risk of being killed by the owner's army of Sicarios.

"She is here, papi. We need to move carefully, eyes are on us," Viola told him.

Bucks wanted to say fuck the eyes, where the hell was his woman, but he was smart enough to see that he would be endangering Paola and Viola if he did. He nodded his head in understanding instead. Paola rubbed his arm, which got his attention.

"Ella va estar bien, papi. She will be okay," she told him once in Spanish and then in English.

One thing Bucks could not understand though was why the hell was his woman in Columbia? And what has she been through being held against her will? Just the thought of the possibilities had Bucks wishing he had a Draco in his hands. He would get all of the answers he needed, then he would go get his woman and leave behind a trail of bloody bodies.

***

Samantha was ready to explode. She was hot! Furious! She was seeing red and her trigger finger was itching. Webster saw he had struck a nerve. He smiled, happy with himself for agitating his wayward wife.

"That bitch knows what I'm capable of! She wants to go against me? I'll kill her!" Samantha exclaimed, so angry that her chest actually started hurting.

"Well. You do have a kill-whoever-you-want-and-get-away-with-it card from that guerilla agency you work for," Webster said, reminding her of her status. "Can't handle it by just sitting here, honey."

"You're right." Samantha got up out of their bed and ran naked into their walk-in closet. Webster held in his laughter as he listened to his wife scramble to get dressed. He was dying for her to leave so he could handle business. Less than five minutes later, Samantha came back out wearing a black vest over a black turtleneck sweater, black leggings and black Puma running shoes. She had a duffle bag in her hand that Webster could tell had something heavy in it.

"I'm surprised you are calling in your little Black boy to do away with Bernice," Webster said, purposely stirring the pot, since he knew T.G. had flown the coop.

"Fuck him! That bitch is mine to kill!" Samantha snapped, grabbing her phone and her keys.

***

A split second later, she was gone, out of the house, hopping into her BMW, and tearing out of the driveway.

Webster watched her turn out onto the street and disappear. Once he was sure his wife was gone, he went out of their bedroom, to one of the guest bedrooms that was on the other side of the house.

"She's gone," he voiced aloud into the dark room.

The light turned on then. There laying on the bed ass naked with a pair of nude-colored pumps on her feet was Bernice, wearing a smile on her face.

"Took long enough," she said, purring nearly. "Can I get what I came for now? My pussy hasn't been worked out in quite some time, Dale."

"It would be my pleasure, ma' lady, especially since my wife doesn't turn me on anymore, but give me a second," Webster told her. "I need to make sure the doors are locked, and the security system is on."

Bernice opened her legs, exposing her wet pussy to him.

"Hurry up. I am not a patient woman, Officer."

***

Webster hurried down the stairs to the first floor then ran to the basement door. He entered and ran down another flight of steps to the main basement. It was a man cave down there. Everything a guy could want in his own personal space to get away from stress, drama and a crazy wife. He went to the bar and made his way behind it. At the center of the liquor shelf, he put his hands on the countertop and pushed down. The lock inside of it disengaged. Webster then reached down to the base of the section and lifted the false part up. The dark tunnel behind it was then revealed. He hurried in and went to the one room that was not in the house's blueprints.

He heard her whimpering. The clanging of chains from her trying to be free made him chuckle. Webster heard her gasp, obviously realizing he was there. Turning the light on, he feasted his eyes on her. She was butt-naked, bound and stuck in the doggy-style position that the kinky sex toy stand kept her in. Red high heels on her feet. Webster floated over to her as if she had a gravitational pull that was too strong for him to resist. The ball gag in her mouth kept her quiet but allowed the sexy lips she had that he kept with red lip gloss on, had a strap that was fastened at the back of her head. Webster ran a hand over her smooth brown skin, along her head. Webster ran a hand over her smooth brown skin, along her left side, to her hip, then he caressed her phat juicy ass.

Dried cum droplets from the last time he had sodomized her remained. His dick grew hard in his Dockers at the memory of her heat.

"Did you miss me?" Webster asked her, his hand sliding from her cheek, to enter her crack, then finger slapping her asshole. She started bucking and kicking at the feeling of his fingernail scratching her inner tract walls. Her pain aroused him. He pulled his finger out and dropped his pants and boxer briefs. Licking his lips, he stroked his cock as he eyed her voluptuous ass that had first hypnotized him when she first appeared with her friend. She wept knowing that he was about to violate her again for the fifth time that day.

"Aww. Don't cry, I'll do my best to be a little bit gentler than I was last time," Webster told her, then positioned himself behind her parted ass, and shoved his cock into her dry brown eye.

She cried out in pain, which aroused him even more. All the years of mental pain that had bruised his ego, he was now getting his revenge, and revenge had never felt so good to him.

"Sorry. I did say I'd do my best," Webster told her, then started laughing like a sick maniac as he violated her, killing her soul even more than he already had.

Chapter 13

Paola and Viola sandwiched Bucks in between them as they danced to a new song by the Brazilian singer, Anitta. Bucks danced along, forcing himself to go along with it. Every few seconds, eyes shifted around, hoping he would catch sight of his woman somehow. Just as his eyes went back to Paola, who was in front of him grinding her ass in his crotch, a man in an expensive pin-striped suit, a clean-shaven bald head with a neatly lined beard approached, flanked by ten other men, all rocking designer labels and custom jewelry. Paolo immediately stopped dancing, when she saw the man. The look on his face gave no inkling of his mood, which scared her.

Bucks stopped dancing, causing Viola to stop. She craned her neck to look around Bucks' wide back. She gasped when she saw the man. Even the crowd of people around them either stopped dancing, stared in shock or moved away.

"Don Jorge," Paola said, trying to hide her shock from the man.

"Que ole, Paola? ¿Quién es este man que estás bailando?" Don Jorge asked, his eyes shifting to Bucks after asking her who is the man she is dancing with.

Paola told the man that Bucks was an urban music promoter from Chicago, and that he was there to party and to possibly scout new talent. Viola corroborated Paola's story, hoping that Don felt no need to check into it.

He nodded his head. "Okay," he said, then looked at Bucks. "It is good to meet you, young man. These, eh, mujeres, eh are 'bery beautiful, verdad?"

"Verdad means 'right'," Viola informed him at his side.

Bucks looked at Don Jorge and nodded. "Very beautiful, sir."

The Don's lips curled into a smile. "Good. Follow me. It is 'bery crowded here, I have VIP room for you and las mujeres. Ven," he said, not asking, but telling.

Bucks looked at Paola and Viola as Don Jorge and his bodyguards turned to leave. Paola looked freaked out, Viola looked afraid.

"Is this the part where things get bloody?" he asked them, dreading the fact that he didn't have a gun.

"No se, papi. I no know why he requests this," Paola replied. "Pero, we no can keep him waiting Just ...be ready," she told him, and started walking.

"Be ready for what?" he asked, seeing the eyes of so many people looking at him as if he was a dead man walking to the chamber.

"Por whatever is to come, papi. Vente," Viola said, then taking his hand she led him on to catch up with Paola and Don Jorge's posse.

**

BANG!

Samantha detonated the small explosive that she had stuck to the front door of Bernice's townhouse. The door shattered to pieces. With her old school SK fitted with a banana clip, Samantha ran in, gun gripped tightly, finger wrapped around the trigger, teeth gritted. Not giving a rat's ass that the residents in the other townhouses likely heard the blast wake them up in the wee hours of the night, she took her time searching the house. Her badge was hanging around her neck, and the top-dog agency she worked for gave her a

"Do-What-The-Fuck-You-Want" pass that would never expire, as long as she handled her business.

Samantha cussed when she came up empty. Bernice wasn't home, but her Mercedes was in its parking space. Pissed, she prepared to head back home when she heard the house phone ringing. Samantha walked over to it and saw the caller I.D., that it was Bernice. She let the voicemail catch the call, not wanting to give up the element of surprise in case Bernice didn't know she was now a target. The sound of Bernice's voice recording came after a final ring.

"You have reached Agent Jaminski. Sorry I missed your call, but if you don't have my cell phone number, that should tell you that I don't fuck with you, so your voice message will not be listed to. Goodbye." Samantha shook her head, then she heard the beep.

"Hello, Sammie."

Samantha's jaw dropped when she heard Bernice address her.

"Oh, come on now, don't look so surprised. You and I are both a little older, but do you really think I wouldn't have cameras in my house that detect the slightest movements? Hell, I knew you were coming before you did! Haa! Anyways, I hope you aren't wearing heels, dear, because you have exactly five seconds to get out or you'll be turned into a giant crispy pork rind. Tah-tah, bitch!"

Samanatha heard rapid beeping then. She shrieked and ran for the front door, just as the explosives Bernice had booby trapped her home with went off. The powerful explosion hurled Samantha right out the front door, landing right on her back, smacking her head on the ground. Dazed from her rattled brain, she saw the massive fire that was the result of the firebomb engulfing Bernice's house.

"Hey! Ma'am! Ma'am! Are you okay?"

A neighbor came over frantically checking on Samatha after he saw her go flying when the house blew up. Samantha sat up and winced from the ricocheting pain in her head. She looked at the burning townhouse again, then she grinded her teeth, infuriated that she had come within seconds of getting cooked by the bitch she knew was soft at heart.

"Ma'am? Do you need me to get you to a hospital?" the guy asked.

Samantha ignored him and managed to get up. As the sounds of sirens from emergency vehicles filled the air, she limped to her car, got in and sped off, leaving the neighbors wondering what in God's name had just happened.

***

Bucks was shocked by how seductive the VIP room was. The red carpet was blood red, wall black with photos and portraits of Don Jorge with some of the most famous singers and rappers in the world, and not just Latinos. It made Bucks think he was in a VIP room at a casino, the way it was furnished and designed. Don Jorge dismissed all but one of the men. After they all left, the one that remained went and closed the door, then he locked it and stood guard. Bucks, standing behind Paola and Viola, looked at the Don. The man looked back at him. Bucks could see that the wheels in Don Jorge's head were turning.

"Si trajiste a este man a mi club para entretenerlo, entonces quiero verla ambos entretenerlo...ahora," he said to Paola and Viola.

Bucks' eyebrows furrowed as he wondered what the hell the old man had just said.

Paola's eyes went wide.

"De que hablas, Don Jorge?" Viola asked, weirded out.

Why the fuck do I not have a gun? I should have just run up on the ol' man's goon and beat him up, take his gun and shot my way up outta this muthafucka, Joe! Bucks thought, until he ended up realizing he was just one of many against everyone who may want to gain favor by the Don, or fill their pockets up with cash.

Don Jorge started smirking at Viola asking what he was talking about, in regards to telling her and Paola that if they brought Bucks to the club to entertain him, then for the both of them to get to it…now.

"¡Quiero veros coger con él ahora mismo! Desnudaos y complace el frente de mi, o asumiré' que habéis traído a un agente federal a mi club y todos moriréis!" he told her.

"Man, what the fuck is this dude sayin'?" Bucks demanded to know.

"He…wants us to fuck you…in front of him or he'll assume that Viola and I brought a fed into his club," Paola informed him.

The Don then dug into the inside of his suit's jacket. Acting out of instinct, Bucks quickly stepped in front of the ladies and shielded them with his own body.

Don Jorge chuckled, seeing the man get protective of the well-known sex club owners. Paola and Viola both grew terrified. They knew exactly what the kingpin was capable of. When he pulled his hand from inside his suit jacket, Bucks saw that Don Jorge had a white plastic Ziploc bag, with a white powdery substance inside. He tossed it onto the table and pointed at it.

"If you are not police," the Don said to Bucks. "Then sniff a line."

Bucks heard the cocking of a gun. He looked back and saw the bodyguard gripping a semi-auto. Paola and Viola ran to the table, dropped down to their knees and hurried to get the bag opened up. Bucks, continuing to eye the Don, sank down to his knees with them. The ladies quickly prepared lines to be snorted. Bucks was reluctant.

"How I know this ain't laced with fentanyl?" he asked Don Jorge.

"We do not destroy our best cash crop with putting poison in it! Now sniff or die!"

Paola knew it was cocaine. This wasn't the first she had heard of the Don testing people, but it was her and Viola's first time being in the hot seat. She went first, snorting up a line. It hit her instantly. The blissful euphoria made her body hum. The sour backdrop that oozed down her throat cleared her nostril and numbed her throat.

Viola grabbed the small golden tooter from Paola and snorted a line. Bucks' hesitation faded, though he was still very reluctant to snort what he sold.

"He will kill us if you don't," Paola told him, pleading to him with her eyes. Bucks took the tooter and inhaled one of the lines. It hit him so hard and so fast that he felt like he wasn't even him anymore. His face got numb, as did his throat. The slime that oozed down his throat made him almost puke, but two seconds after, he felt a warm energetic sensation inside of him. His dick grew hard on its own. His mind raced, his heart pounded in his chest.

"Muy bien," Don Jorge said with a sadistic grin. He sat on the couch across from his jacket, he pulled out a big cigar with a gold zippo. He made a motion to the ladies to get on with it, then flamed up his Cohiba.

"Papi, I sorry, pero we have to do—"

"It's cool." Bucks cut her off and stood. "He wants a show, fuck it, we'll give him one."

He took their hands, helped them up from the floor. Paola started undoing Bucks' pants, getting aroused when she realized his dick was already hard. Viola helped him out of his shirt, then joined Paola in front of him as she dropped his pants and boxer briefs down to his ankles, freeing his pulsating dick.

"Chupalo, mujeres," Don Jorge told them, after he exhaled a cloud of smoke.

The two dropped down before Bucks. The cocaine had them both in overdrive. Both of them had watery mouths at the sight of his nine-inch pipe. Paola opened her mouth wide and slowly engulfed him, while Viola went to take his balls into her mouth.

"Oohhh, sh-sh-shhheeeeit!! Bucks groaned as the sensational bliss of two wet mouths pleasing him, combined with the cocaine charging him up, had him feeling like he could take off like Superman.

***

Bernice looked at him. He was out like a broken light bulb. To be sure, she patted his face. "Dale?"
PAT! PAT! PAT!
"Hey. Wake up," she said to him.
Webster didn't move. He just snored his ass off. Benice pushed up one of his eyelids. Still no movement. She let his lid go and smirked to herself. The strong sleep agent she had spiked the glass of cognac with had done the trick. The minute she sucked all of his cum out of his dick, Webster passed right out and had not moved an inch. Bernice took a deep breath to calm her rapidly beating heart, then she hurried off the bed and put her clothes back on. Right after she put her socks and her Nike running shoes on, she grabbed her tote bag, keys to her car and crept out of the room.

***

As quietly as she could, she followed her phone's step tracker app that had recorded Webster's movements earlier that evening. She had placed a small device in his back pockets that was accurate enough to show where he had walked. Her heart pounded like drums at an African tribe ritual as she got down to the basement. She turned all the lights on and looked around at the man cave. Nothing looked out of the ordinary. She looked at her phone again, the recording displayed he had gone through a tunnel at the east end of the basement. Bernice looked at the east wall but saw only the bar there. Automatically, she was sure that Webster had the tunnel hidden somewhere behind it.

She hurried behind the bar, and looked it all over, trying to find the most likely way to open the passageway up. After nearly ten grueling minutes of pulling bottles of liquor, trying beer dispensing levers, the damn water faucet knobs, Bernice was ready to give up on finding who she knew was there. She rested her hands on the countertop, at the center of the bar, muttering a curse, when suddenly she heard the sound of something disengaging.

The section she had put her hands on slightly lifted. Bernice gasped. Taking a wild guess, she pushed the countertop in, but it didn't move. She tried to pull it to herself but still nothing. Then she went to lift it up and the section began rising up like a tiny storage room door. The dark tunnel was then revealed. Bernice shrieked excitedly and hurried in and made it to the secret room seconds later.

She got her iPhone out and turned on the flashlight app to see inside. She saw her, tied down on some sort of contraption that had her in the doggy-style position. Gasping, Bernice hurried to find the room's light switch. When she turned it on, her heart dropped when she saw the naked and battered Illinois State Police Sergeant there, with red heels on her feet, and bruises on her body and face.

"Jones! Oh, God!"

Bernice ran to Yvette. She was barely conscious and barely breathing. Bernice shook her, calling her name repeatedly. Yvette groaned, her eyes squinting as she winced in pain.

"Hey! Jones! Come on, wake up! I'm gonna get you outta here!" Bernice swore to her.

It was then that she realized that Yvette had been drugged, just by how red and dilated her eyes were, and she was likely dehydrated, due to how pale her skin was. Bernice went to undo the strap to her left wrist, when she heard the sound that was the worst possible at such a dire moment.

Click Clack!

"You really are a fool, Bernice," she heard Webster say. "See I was in the military, before I became a cop. I am an expert at playing dead and at playing sleep. Now, turn around, very slowly, or I'll shoot you in your ass."

Bernice complied. Slowly as directed, she turned around and faced where Webster was standing, pointing a Taurus Judge revolver at her. Bernice's bladder let go. She pissed all down the inside of her leggings, urine pooling inside her sneakers.

"Awww. Did you just tinkle on yourself?" Webster teased.

"Just…just let her go, Dale. This has gone far enough," Bernice said. "Your obsession with her had you acting like a crazed—"

POW!

Webster pulled the trigger.

"Aaaaaagggggghhhh!" Bernice screamed, as her right knee was blown completely off. She fell to the floor, her stump gushing blood while her blown-off leg leaked more.

***

Webster watched his wife's former co-agent/partner in crime bleed out, screaming in agony, trying to hold in the blood from spewing out. He glanced up at Yvette, and saw she was moaning, struggling against the restraints that held her on all fours, but still way too weak from the heroin concoction he had injected her with, after he raped her rear end again. Bernice's screaming and crying brought his eyes back to her. He curled his lip up, disgusted with how much of a dirty bitch she was.

"You son of a bitch! You're dead, motherfucker! Deeeaaad!" Bernice screamed at him.

POW!

Like a tried-n-true Western gunslinger, Webster whipped the revolver's barrel up, aiming at her head and blew it completely to pieces, silencing Bernice forever.

"Shut up, you fucking cunt," he said, sneering at the bleeding headless corpse.

Yvette groaned. The noise caught his attention. The ball-gag in her mouth was still preventing her from speaking. He looked at where Bernice had dropped her tote bag. Going to it, he picked it up and fished her iPhone out of it. He swiped the screen and was amazed to see that she didn't have a security access code to be entered. He unlocked the phone, and almost immediately saw that Bernice had been transmitting a signal. Someone was tracking her, and at any time they could be arriving.

"Guess we gotta re-locate, Jones," Webster said, walking up behind Yvette and smacking her juicy ass. "Don't worry, though, we'll go somewhere really nice this time of the year, where nobody will ever bother us. Now let me go get you some sleepy time juice. Wouldn't want to ruin the surprise of where we're going." He smacked her ass cheek again, then went to where he had a stash of dope/sedative shots at the bar, ready to keep his sex slave under an unbreakable spell.

Chapter 14

"Fuuck!" Bucks groaned, as Paola bounced up and down on his dick, while he felt Viola licking his nuts. The lounge chair he was laid on was reclined. Paola was stripped of her tiny top, breasts bouncing as she did, skirt up around her waist, dick up inside of her, stilettos still on her feet, and her mouth opened wide as she moaned so loudly from the bliss of Black dick.

Viola, no top, skirt up, heels on, could tell Paola was so close to cumming. She leaked and dripped down Bucks' pole, drenching him like her pussy was water-boarding his crotch. Viola smacked Paola's ass, then she soaked her middle finger in Paola's juices. She then stuck her finger right inside of Paola's asshole, which made Paola moan louder. Bucks groaned louder, feeling Paola's pussy muscles clench around his joint. The Columbiana had him so close to busting his nut, and did not want to pull out. In his peripheral, he saw Don Jorge was still watching. His cigar sat in an ashtray, still smoldering. The man's face was unreadable.

"Aayy!" cried out Paola, then she came, all over Bucks' dick.

"Ahora cambium!" Don Jorge demanded of them.

"Switch, papi," Paola told Bucks, then managed to climb up off him.

Viola got up on the lounger, positioning herself on all fours. She lowered her face, tooted her ass up high. Paola grabbed her ass cheeks and after she parted them, opening Viola up wide, she spit a wad of saliva onto Viola's puckered asshole, Paola took Bucks' dick into her hand and put the tip of it to Viola's crack. She lubed her asshole up, rubbing it all around with Bucks' dick, she then spit on Bucks' dick, before inserting his cock into Viola's butthole.

Bucks groaned, eyes closing as the tight warmth of her enveloped him. Viola squealed from how good it hurt. She glanced up and saw Don Jorge staring right at her still wearing a poker face. Bucks fucked Viola's asshole and filled her with blissful pleasure. It was so good that he completely forgot that Don Jorge was watching the whole thing along with his bulldog at the door. He damn near even forgot why he was in Colombia in the first place.

Minutes later, Viola exploded again, cumming all over Bucks' thighs. He kept thrusting in and out, groaning and cursing, nut rising. Viola grabbed his dick, pulled him out, then opened her mouth wide as she sank down to her knees. Paola hurried to follow suit. Side by side, the two eagerly awaited to taste Bucks. He growled and groaned, jerking his dick in their faces. Ten seconds later, Bucks busted his nut.

Paola and Viola slurped and guzzled down all of his semen, then they started kissing each other, swapping spit and cum with each other. It was so dirty and nasty and freaky that Bucks wished he had more nut to bust so he could watch them do it again.

Clapping then came. They all looked and saw Don Jorge standing up, giving them all applause for their very entertaining performance.

"Maravilloso, mi gente! ¡Absolutamente maravilloso!" he cheered. Looking at Bucks, he then spoke English. "You, young man, should be a worker at estas damas club, you would please lots of ladies. Pero, I wonder if your fiancée will still marry you, if you fucked ten or more ladies per day."

Buck's eyes went wide in shock. He was instantly rendered speechless by the Don knowing that he was engaged. Paola and Viola both went rigid with fear as Don Jorge started smirking at them all.

"Si, Señor Bernard Hernz. I know who you are and why you have come to my country. Let us see what your Vietnamese wife thinks of you having a threesome with two well-known whores."

Just then, Bucks heard the sound of someone sobbing. Paola and Viola heard it as well. They looked around to see where it was coming from. Directly behind them, on the screen on a massive HDTV screen that was the size of the wall it had been built into, Bucks saw his future wife's face, with tears running down from her eyes.

"Julie! Baby!" Bucks shouted, beyond relieved, yet horrified that she had likely just seen him piping the Colombian freaks down. "I'm here! I came to bring you home!"

Paola and Viola looked at Bucks' woman. They felt horrible. They could see she was sitting, but not much else.

"How could you do that, Bucks?" Julie asked as her voice broke up.

"Baby, I had to!"

"He is lying to you!" Don Jorge stepped over to where Bucks stood, still naked, "Nobody put a gun to his head. He does not love you."

Bucks looked at the Don. He grew furious at the man's blatant bullshit.

"Don Jorge!" Paola cried. "Por favor, señor! Dejala ir! Ella es el amor de su Viola! No se merece esto!"

"Callate, perra!" the Don snapped, then went to grab her.

Bucks caught Don Jorge and hemmed the man up in a tight head lock.

The bodyguard pulled his pistol out and shouted for Bucks to release him or die.

"Fuck you! Drop yo' gun or I'll snap this bitch ass nigga's neck!" Bucks shouted back.

"Bucks!" Julie panicked, seeing her fiancé making a very deadly mistake. "What are you doing?!"

"I'm showin' this fake ass Pablo Escobar what a real gangsta looks like!"

Bucks was about to put the squeeze on the Don's neck and suffocate him, while the bodyguard kept his gun trained on Bucks, and the ladies stood to the side, scared to death, the camera moved from Julie's face and landed on one that made Bucks jaw drop and his eyes go wide in shock.

"What up, my nigga?" said Rueben, with a diabolical smirk on his face. "Check it out, fam. That's my dad you got in a headlock. I'ma need you to let him go or…"

The camera zoomed out, so that Rueben and Julie were both on the screen. Rueben then pulled out a Glock and put it to Julie's head.

"Aye, man!" Bucks shouted, fearing the worst.

"All that hollerin' ain't necessary. Let my pops go. He lookin' a little blue right now."

Bucks saw the terrified look in his woman's eyes. He let Don Jorge go, reluctantly, then the bodyguard rushed over to take the boss and pull him behind him.

"Now this what's gon' happen, bro. You and them thot-ianas go come over here, and we gon' talk. You made a really big mistake comin' to my country without my permission. But before yo' ass gets over here, please put cho' clothes on. Don't nobody want to see that shit, my nigga. Hurry up, too." The screen went black then. Bucks stood there for a minute, feeling like he was stuck to the floor. Paola and Viola were in tears, terrified like never before.

Don Jorge cleared his throat, then he looked at the three. His eyes rolled to Bucks a second later. He smirked, then chuckled. "My son es muy loco, Senor Hernz," the Don told Bucks, "and you pissed him off. Ahora, put your clothes on, and move."

"Ahora! Muevete!" the bodyguard shouted, pointing his gun right at Bucks' face. Bucks obeyed. As he got dressed and put his shoes back on, Paola and Viola followed suit. Don Jorge went and retrieved a gold AK-47 from behind the bar. The bodyguard gestured for the ladies to start walking and for Bucks to follow them. He and Don Jorge fell in behind the three, both of them itching to lay them all down the second they got the chance to.

***

Arriving at a big wooden door, down in an old concrete tunnel that looked so ancient from the rusted minecarts littering it, the bodyguard banged on the door twice, then waited. The door opened five seconds later to the sound of skin smacking and groaning. Bucks was forced inside first. He immediately saw Rueben, gripping the hips of a woman that was tied up and bent over a chair, fucking her hard and fast from the back. The further he stepped in, Bucks gasped in horror when he realized that it was his pregnant fiancée getting violated by the Colombian thug.

"No! Bae!"

Bucks attempted to rush up on Rueben.

WHAM!

A bat came flying from the left, hitting him in his sternum. All of the wind was knocked out of him. He fell to the cold hard concrete floor, gasping for air.

"Hold up, my nigga!" he heard Rueben groan. "I'm almost done! Woo! Damn, yo' wife got some bomb-ass pussy, fam!"

Paola and Viola were completely horrified by the foul act. Neither of them could even form words. Bucks tried to get up, but when three AK-47s were pointed at him, he had no choice but to stay where he was. A pair of hands then grabbed him. As if he weighted one hundred pounds less than he was, Bucks was hoisted up and turned towards the direction of his girl being raped.

Julie cried her eyes out, pleading for Rueben to stop. She had heard the door open, then her man shout in panic for her, right before the sound of him being struck by something and put on the ground. Then she heard the sounds of assault rifles cocking, which meant the brutal torture was far from over. Bucks couldn't watch. He felt so powerless, his future wife that was carrying their child in her belly was being violated just ten feet in front of him

He closed his eyes and tried to block out the sounds of Julie crying in pain.

SMACK!

A fiery hot pain from an open hand made Bucks' face burn.

"No cierres los ojos, puto! ¡Quiero que veas a tu mujer siendo cojida en su culo!" he heard Don Jorge say.

"Yeah, bro!" grunted Rueben, pulling his dick out of Julie's pussy. "Watch me fuck yo' bitch in her ass! This shit gon' be dope!"

***

The gag in Julie's mouth muffled her blood-curdling scream when Rueben rammed his dick into her asshole. It hurt her to the point that she felt like she was going to pass out. Rueben grabbed her hair and yanked her head back while he pulverized her anus. He grunted, cursed and taunted her fiancé. Julie found herself begging for death right at that moment. She knew if she somehow made it out of this alive, Bucks would never respect, nor would he continue to love her. She would be deemed "trash," and he would throw her out of his life to be picked up and taken away by men that loved trashy women.

Julie then heard females begging the old Colombian in Spanish to stop his son. The man laughed and cheered his son on.

These mutherfuckers are sick! What the fuck? Julie thought, as Rueben started going harder, pushing himself all the way up her ass. Never in her life had Julie felt so powerless and hopeless. She felt so low that even the ground was up higher. Then, sheer will to get herself and her future hubby up out of there, one way or another kicked into gear. There was nothing she wouldn't do to save him and their unborn child.

Jule took a deep breath, then started pushing. She pushed harder and harder, and harder until she forced her bowels to explode, all over Rueben's dick.

"Aaawww, what the fuuuuck!" Rueben shouted, jumping back and looking down at his shit-covered cock. "This bitch just shit on me, Joe!"

***

Right after he saw Rueben jump back, yanking his dookie dick out of Julie, Paola and Viola threw all caution to the wind and rushed two of the men that were pointing choppers at him. They both jumped on the guards and were able to take them down to the floor. Bucks acted quickly as the girls dug their fingers into the men's eyes, inflicting so much pain on the two that they released their guns. He grabbed the AK that Don Jorge was just turning to blast Paola and Viola and yanked hard enough that it made the Don fall to the ground, landing right next to him.

CRACK! BAM! CRACK!

Bucks rocked the old man's jaw, then head-butted him hard in the nose, breaking it then socked Don Jorge again, knocking him clean out. Bucks saw Paola and Viola still trying to rip the two guys' eyes out. He looked for his woman, but she wasn't bent over the couch anymore. Movement in his peripheral caught his attention. He saw Rueben then, dragging Julie by her bound wrist out of the dungeon door.

"Shit! JuJu!" he shouted, hopping up from the ground. Bucks staggered to get to the door, head still throbbing and bleeding from the gaping wound in the back. Seconds before he reached the doorway, the door was slammed shut.

"Nooo!" Bucks tried to open it, turning the knob, pushing on the door at the same time, trying to barge his way through, but his efforts were futile. "Fuuuuuuck! You punk bitch rapist muthafucka! I swear to God, I'ma chop yo' dick off and make you eat it, pussy!"

Bucks heard laughing coming from the other side of the door just then.

"Shut cho' bitch ass up! Just for sayin' that weird-ass shit, I'ma take yo' nasty-ass wife, clean her up then I'ma fuck her all up in her ass again! And if she shit on me again, I'ma make my donkey fuck her! Peace out, payaso!"

Bucks continued trying to get the door open, but it wouldn't budge.

BRRRRRRRRR!

BRRRRRRRRR!

Deafening AK-47 blasts ricocheted off the wall inside the room. Bucks turned his head and saw that Paola and Viola had the two guards' choppers in their hands and had blown their faces off. Don Jorge was just coming to from his unconscious state, when they pointed at him. He opened his eyes and saw the two aiming at him. He sneered at them, with bloody teeth.

"Estan muertos, putas! Y tus families van a mor—"

BRRRRRRRRRRRRRRRRR!

BRRRRRRRRRRRRRRRRR!

More than thirty shots from each chopper turned the kingpin into chunks of bloody meat, splattered all over the floor.

"Puta!" Paola spat at the scattered pieces.

Viola looked back at Bucks. She saw him leaned against the door, looking as if he had given up.

"Papi…" With tears, Viola went to him. "No te preocupes. Will get tu mujer back to you. I promise to you."

"There's no way out. We're stuck," Bucks told her, then slid down to the floor. "That creep-ass nigga, Joe. I coulda' had his bitch ass."

Paola came to Viola's side. Neither of them knew what to do, or to say, but one thing that they did know was that it was not looking good.

***

Just then from somewhere in the building, the three heard a very loud explosion. It was powerful enough that the whole room shook like an earthquake was happening. Paola and Viola both looked up at the ceiling. Bucks opened his eyes and looked up.

"What the hell was that?" he wondered.

No sooner than he had asked it, did the sounds of machine guns and assault rifles come, making it sound like a war had just popped off, right above their heads.

***

"You's a nasty bitch, shortie. I can't believe you really dookied on my dick. Fuck is wrong with you? I should slap the fuck out cho' ass, bitch," said Rueben, dragging his Vietnamese prisoner behind him by the rope tied around her wrists. "Then you did that shit in front of yo' bitch ass boyfriend, too. You know his ass don't want you no more. I should've made you suck my dick in front of him, but yo crazy ass would've bit my shit off, I bet."

Not only is this dude a straight up creep ass bitch…his ass don't know how to shut the fuck up. Booooy, I'm tellin' you, if I get the chance…his ass gon' scream like Mariah Carey's loud-ass, Joe, thought Julie, as the gag in her mouth prevented her from telling him to shut the fuck up.

145

BOOM!

A sudden explosion rocked the ground under them. Dust and dirt fell from the tunnel's ceiling as it slightly cracked.

"The hell was that?" Rueben asked, looking up at the ceiling, as the lights flickered.

He then heard gunshots come from above. His eyes went wide as so many different scenarios filled his head. He got so preoccupied that when Julie pulled her move out of sheer desperation to live and save her family, Rueben was caught completely off guard.

With all of her pissed and pregnant might, Julie yanked her bound wrists hard enough to jerk Rueben downwards. A split second later, she rolled back and shot her legs up. Her feet slammed into his face. He flew backwards and landed on his ass. Julie catapulted herself up from the ground, ignoring the pain that hit her like a jolt of electricity. Before Rueben could get up, she pounced on him and started pounding on his face with the bottoms of her fists.

"Aaghh! Get the fuck off me, you crazy hoe!" Rueben shouted, trying to block his face from her furious hands.

CRACK! CRACK! CRACK! CRACK! CRACK!

She pummeled Rueben's face, drawing blood, swelling him up, screaming at the top of her lungs. Rueben countered her fury with his own. He shot a right jab up to her jaw, rocking her so hard that she flew backwards and hit her head against the ground.

"Fuuck!" she screamed in pain, her eyes seeing two of everything she looked at.

"Dumbass bitch!" Rueben jumped on her and wrapped his hands around her neck. "Die, bitch! You and yo' fuckin' baby! Diiiee!"

Julie grabbed at his hands, trying to pry them from her throat. She couldn't breathe and was quickly beginning to see spots. He squeezed harder, looking down at her, fiending to watch the light in her eyes turn off.

Her life flashed before her eyes. So many memories…good, bad, horrible, life changing, she saw Yvette, her best friend, and secret lover, she saw Bucks, the love of her life. She saw Lieutenant Michaels and Lieutenant Sikes, Sir and Rock, Eric and Bunz.

Tears welled up in her eyes as it dawned on her that it was over…

BOCKA! BOCKA! BOCKA! BOCKA!

BOCKA! BOCKA! BOCKA! BOCKA!

Gunshots rang out randomly as Julie's vision began fading. She felt warm liquid spatter on her face. A second later, Rueben fell to the side and he didn't get up.

"Julie!"

She heard the voice, but she swore that there was no way it could be him. She figured she did die.

She felt herself being pulled up from the ground a second later. When her eyes came into focus, she discovered that she was not suffering hallucinations from lack of oxygen in her brain from nearly being strangled to death. She was looking at the face of the man that was the reason she was in Colombia, sold to the high-level cocaine lords as a sex toy, while her best friend was somewhere else, likely suffering the same horrors.

"You!" Julie snapped as blind fury filled her in an instant, but she was still too weak to grab and choke him out.

***

T.G. saw nothing but pure malice in Julie's eyes. He already knew he would, though he half-expected bullets to wet him up the way he had just done Rueben.

"Yes, JuJu. It's me, I know how badly I fucked up and I will suffer the consequences very soon I'm sure, but right now, we gotta get you outta here before this bitch ass nigga's army gets here," T.G. urged her.

"I'm not leaving without Bucks, you snake-ass bitch!" Julie swore, with both fire and ice in her eyes.

T.G.'s heart dropped when he heard her say his roadie's name. His jaw dropped at that.

"B-Bucks is…here?"

"Yeah, he is, bitch! He knows what you did too. Where the fuck is Yvette?" she then demanded to know.

"W-What? She's...not with you?" T.G. asked, having thought the entire time that they had been sent off together.

He heard the sound of footsteps before Julie could reply. Quickly, he turned, putting her behind him and aimed his twin FN five sevens, both of them still with plenty more shots in their custom extended, double-stack clips. Fingers wrapped around the triggers, T.G. got ready to dump on whoever came around the corner from where he had come from, searching high and low for Julie and Yvette, based off of the info given to him by the guard he had come within seconds of shooting his jaw off.

The footsteps got louder. T.G. went stiff. He prayed that if nothing else, before he died that he could get Julie out of there. Three seconds later, he saw the cavalry had arrived. Instant relief washed over him, when he saw ChaCha and Danny come around the corner gripping their fully automatic .50 caliber weapons of mass fuck the opps in their hands. Right behind the Valdez family queen and kin, were the two Valdez family princes/Steel City Mafia goons, Macho and his brother Tool, both of the dread heads gripping big M249s, as well as four fitted with 200-round ammunitions boxes, and all four of them wearing Kevlar.

ChaCha saw Julie and screamed with excitement. She ran to her, pushing T.G. away and hurrying to untie her wrists and ankles.

"She said Bucks is here," T.G. told the other three.

Macho and Tool still wore glares of pure hatred for T.G. on their faces. Danny, older and more equipped mentally to handle dirty deeds with a poker face, looked at T.G. and nodded.

"We know. He's somewhere down here, too," he replied calmly, though secretly boiling inside.

"He's in the dungeon that dude's bitch ass had me in!" Julie sobbed, now free of her restraints.

ChaCha quickly took her vest and shirt off and helped Julie into them, giving her some type of cover. Now only in a sports bra, with her army fatigue cargos and steel toe boots on, ChaCha picked her gun back up and was back in murder mode.

"Lead the way, JuJu. We need to move fast," she said, knowing how the Colombian army got down for those that paid the most.

***

Bucks, Paola and Viola all pointed their choppers at the door, getting ready to try and blast their way out when they all heard Julie yelling Buck's name from the outside.

"JuJu!" he hollered back, standing right at the door.

It unlocked a second later, then opened. Bucks didn't have the chance to do it first. Julie ran right into his arms and cried her eyes out. Bucks couldn't help it either. His emotions got away from him. He broke down and cried with her, overjoyed that his fiancée was actually back in his arms.

Bucks was careful not to squeeze her too tightly. Their child was inside her, and he knew that without a doubt, her body was broken up. Paola and Viola felt the heavy weight that had been on their chests lift and fade. They saw the other people that Julie had come with. They both gasped when they saw the notorious Arctic blue-eyed Colomborriquena killer queen pin.

"Dios Mio…no puedo creerlo!" Paola said to herself, bewildered that Ximena "ChaCha" Sandoval Valdez was there. Viola was speechless. Period.

Bucks looked up from having buried his face in the corner of her neck and saw ChaCha, her passive husband, Macho and Tool. He was filled with gratitude for their help but was puzzled as to how they were there. He had not contacted them. Hell, he didn't even know he would be getting sent to South America to get his woman back, so he couldn't for the life of him figure out how they knew where he or Julie was. Then, behind the four of them, Bucks saw him. He was there. With them.

Julie felt her man tighten up just then, turning as hard as a rock. *Oh, shit* ... she thought, knowing that Bucks seen T.G.

***

T.G. locked eyes with the man that had been his best friend and partner for more years than either of them could remember. Now, they were enemies, adversaries, opps. Nothing between them but bloodshed and death was possible now.

Just as he knew, Bucks let go of Julie and tried rushing at him. Danny and Macho caught him, though, stopping him.

"You bitchass nigga! Yo ass dead, Joe! On my baby, nigga!"

T.G. couldn't blame Bucks. He knew he was bogus as hell for what he did.

"I'm ...I'm sorry, bro," T.G. said, trying to keep his emotions in check.

"Fuck yo' sorry, bitch-nigga!" Bucks yelled, still trying to get past the muscular men that were actually having a hard time holding him back.

ChaCha was dying to see T.G. get his teeth kicked in. She was from Jackson Heights. New Yorkers did not tolerate snakes. Julie was ready to get on T.G.'s ass herself, to ride with her man and fuck that nigga all the way up!

"Bucks," ChaCha said, stepping over to him, touching his shoulder. "We need to go, papa. Trust me, you will get your chance, but right now isn't the time."

"His ass gon' run if I don't catch him now, ChaCha!"

"Naw, bro, I'm not runnin'," T.G. swore. "I am gonna' take what comes like a man. I deserve nothing' for what I did."

Bucks was halfway shocked by what T.G. said. He wasn't expecting him to be ready to man up.

"Yeah, aight, nigga! We gon' see, Joe! On God, we gon see!" Bucks declared, venomously glaring at T.G.

***

Julie turned and looked at the red-haired and pink-haired Colombian women. While ChaCha talked Bucks off the edge of murderous fury so they could get up out of there, she walked up to them.

"Where is Yvette?" she demanded to know.

"Who?" the redhead asked, with puzzled brows.

Julie shook her head. The worst fucking feeling ever was in the pit of her stomach as it became obvious that Yvette was not there, maybe not even in Columbia.

"Thank you for helping my fiancé. I really appreciate you both," Julie then told them.

The girl with the pink hair nodded. "He is a good man."

CRACK!

Julie cocked back and plowed her jaw, sending her to the ground.

The redhead shrieked when Julie swung on her.

WHAM!

Down she went, joining her friend, rubbing her jaw. Neither of them attempted to get up.

"JuJu? What the hell?" Bucks asked, hurrying to grab her before she tore Paola and Viola up.

151

"I should knock your ass out, too, goddamit! You put your dick in those bitches, Bernard!"

"Aye!" ChaCha shouted then. ¡Tenemos que ir ahora mismo! Shut the fuck up and let's move!"

"Asshole," Julie snuck in at Bucks, then turned on her bare feet to leave out of the room. Cocking back and punching T.G. in his jaw, she stepped out.

"Boooooy, yo' lady is a muthafuckin' G, my nigga!" said Macho, with a giant grin on his face.

"Don't I know it," Bucks replied, helping Paola and Viola up from the ground. "Sorry 'bout that, ladies. My lady is mean when she's angry."

"And so is mine if y'all muthafuckaz don't 'hurr up and get goin'," Danny chimed in, looking at how angry his blue-eyed skull-cracker wife looked because they were still talking and not moving.

Bucks ushered Paola and Viola out, mean-mugging T.G. as he rubbed his jaw. They hurried to catch up with Julie, while the others hurried behind them, ready to get out of there, and go find Yvette.

Chapter 15

Days Later ...

Denise cried her eyes out after Charlise had stopped by to bring her a manila envelope full of papers that T.G. had drawn up, naming her as the owner of his luxury rental and chauffeur car service, and including his share in a few stocks that he had made some investments in. He had even put her name on the bank accounts, which were just a few digits short of looking like phone numbers.

Charlise was on the brink of tears. A random text message from an unknown number had hit her phone a few days prior. The words she saw she knew were from her cousin. Without them actually saying it, she knew that T.G. would not be returning.

"Why?" Denise cried, distraught over the meaning of T.G. relinquishing his business, stocks, and account to her. "Why couldn't he just stay?"

Charlise reached out to her and hugged her. She was aware of what her cousin had done. It was indeed foul to her, but she was a southern woman through and through. She was raised to ride for family whether they were right or dead-ass wrong. She didn't have the heart to tell Denise what T.G. had done, though she was very sure that the young mother was in love with him to the point, Denise probably wouldn't give a rat's ass about T.G.s past, as long as they could have a great future together.

"Tremaine...he's..." Charlise just could not figure out what to say, without breaking down as well.

"He was so good with Letoya," Denise wept. "I can't believe he's not comin' back."

Charlise did her best to comfort Denise, but she knew that when a good woman found what she felt was a good man, then lost him, not much could bring back the happy unless you brought back the man.

***

Denise hugged Charlise then let her out of the new condominium that she had been also given by T.G. She went and got her daughter from her crib, gave Letoya a breast feeding, bathed her then dressed her, before getting herself showered and ready for her day. She slid her voluptuous body into a stylish Max Mara maxi-dress, banana yellow with red bow-tie ribbons all over it. It was backless, with a tear-dropped shaped opening just above her breasts, long sleeves and a ruffled triple hemline that stopped just above her knees. Her legs, freshly waxed and oiled, glistened. On her feet, she slid on spike-toed Christian Louboutins that matched the form-fitting dress. Her dreads hung loosely down her shoulders. She applied dark red eyeshadow and black eyeliner, dark red lipstick, gold jewelry, then spritzed on some Dior perfume.

She checked herself in the mirror and almost smiled when she saw the beautiful Haitian woman looking back at her. But wishing T.G. was there, holding her with his strong arms against his hard body, made tears well up in her eyes. She closed them, then spoke. "Tanpri, Bondye. Kembe Tremaine an sekirite. Kelkwswa Kote I ye Kaunye a tampri, kenbe I an sekirite, epi kite I tounen vin jwenn nou," she prayed in her native Haitian Creole tongue, asking God to keep T.G. safe, wherever he was at the moment, and to bring him back to her and Letoya.

Denise opened her eyes, took a deep breath to gather herself. She had goals now. She wanted to be a contributing factor in T.G. 's business booking, to honor him. Maybe he would hear about it and come back.

***

She got Letoya into the car seat of the Maybach S580 and hopped in behind the wheel. Rolling off, Denise put on some music. Victoria Monet's "On My Mama" began crooning from the Burmester surround sound audio system, filling the exclusive big body double M Benz with real music.

Thirty-odd minutes later, she turned into the expansive business' lot, just half a mile away from the airport. It boasted an enormous parking section that was covered by custom outdoor roofing to protect the multi-billion-dollar inventory of cars and SUVs.

Denise parked at the main door to the office and got out, got the baby stroller from the trunk, and got Letoya out of the back of the car, putting her in the stroller. Entering the office, Denise was greeted by a few of the office personnel and one of the chauffeurs. She acknowledged them all with enthusiastic salutations. The office manager, a buxom belle with ebony skin and her hair cut down into a fade, with designs edged in on one side, headed towards Denise from her office. The heels of her stiletto boots clacked loudly as she strutted with a fast-paced walk in her tight burgundy wrap dress. Denise saw the worrisome expression the woman had on her face. She made her way to meet Patrice halfway.

"Hey, umm, Denise. I got...there was somethin' in the mail I picked up that, uh...you should come see this," Patrice told her.

"Okay? Lead the way."

Denise pushed the stroller, following behind Patrice. They entered her office. Patrice closed the door, then went to her desk where a stack of mail sat next to the big Apple computer monitor. Patrice picked up a brown legal envelope and gave it to Denise. Opening it, Denise glanced at Patrice, peeping how nervous the woman was. She pulled the piece of paper out of the envelope, and gasped when she saw a full-size photo of T.G. and Letoya enjoying a chicken and waffle dinner at the Twisted Soul Cookhouse G-Pours restaurant. A circle in red marker was drawn around them. The word's "I see you....BANG! BANG!" were under it, with a winking smiley face to top it off.

Denise gasped. "Oh my God!"

"Boss," Patrice then said.

Denise looked at her, with fright etched into her face.

"When I got here…there was a black Lincoln exiting out, coming from where the envelope was left."

Her heart dropped out of her ass.

"She knows! Samantha knows I'm alive! Shhit!" Denise panicked.

"What's going on, Denise? Are you in trouble?"

Denise nodded her head.

"Well." Patrice pulled one of her desk drawers open and got her Glock 19 out. "Then whoever that is tryna' start some shit, they got to get through me, to get to you and that angelic little thang."

Looking at the statuesque woman, Denise somehow managed to muster up a smile, though in no way shape or form, did she have confidence that anyone in her life had the means, nor the capability to stop Samantha once she was locked on to a target, and hell bent on eliminating it.

***

Bucks had a smile on his face that was as big as the Mississippi River. With his head resting on her belly, on top of their growing child, nothing could have made him happier. After a thorough series of doctor's appointments that came within a few days of being in a hospital, it was assured to Bucks and Julie that their baby was safe, and strong.

Having his daily back home meant the world to him. There had not been a day where he had let her out of his sight, out of fear that if he did, she would disappear again Laid up in the massive canopy topped bed, in their lavish glass-ceiling master bedroom, Bucks and Julie relaxed with each other, while watching Chicago's WGN News.

Seconds after the gorgeous traffic reporter Bhrett Vickery gave a run down on travel time in and around Chi-Town, another segment detailing devastating news of Kamala Harris' defeat in the presidential candidacy.

"This shit crazy, Joe. Bitch ass crackerjack caught a sex case, incited a riot, is a known racist, decrees abortion to be criminal, and he claims he didn't know that Kamala was Black?" Bucks said, as the old man's face appeared on their gigantic 4K HDTV.

"People gon' regret this for a looong time," Julie said, shaking her head.

The sounds of puppy barks made them both look towards the doorway to the bedroom. The four-month-old male Dogo Argentino pup ran into the room, full speed. Bucks and Julie watched the all-white Argentinian Mastiff attempt to jump up on the bed but only got his front paws and chin up on the edge. Julie giggled and Bucks rolled over to pick the new addition to their family up. The pup started prancing around excitedly, commanding their attention, making them both laugh their asses off at the clipped-eared future demon.

"I miss Rock so much, bae," Julie said forlornly. "He was my world."

Bucks nodded his head, already knowing how much she had adored her German Shepherd. Julie and Yvette both got Rock and Sir at the same time and had raised them themselves. The attachment they had with their dogs was as much as a shepherd had with his or her livestock. They provided for each other and took care of each other.

"I miss him too, love," said Bucks, giving the pup a belly rub while he laid on his back. "But now we got Jarvis Jr. to raise and train into a beast."

Julie smiled. She loved how Bucks had been the one to suggest naming their puppy after Lieutenant Michaels. When she had been told about his death, Julie broke like a glass cup being dropped on concrete. It was devastating to lose the closest thing to a father that she and Yvette ever had. It made the way Rueben was killed seem way too nice. If she had it her way, Rueben would have been turned into dog food for what he did.

"Jarvis, come here, baby." Julie patted her side and giggled as Jarvis Jr. hopped up and hurried to plop down at her side. "That's my baby! You are so cute!"

Bucks repositioned himself alongside his fiancée, so that Jarvis Jr. was in between them. Julie picked the pup up and set him on Bucks' sternum, then put her man's arm around her as she cuddled up with him. Bucks held her tightly to him, content with life. But still, in the back of his mind and Julie's, they were still missing a big part of their lives.

"Bucks! Bucks!"

Their vibe was put on hold when Paola appeared in the doorway. Bucks could feel Julie tense up. She was not exactly thrilled about Paola and Viola living in their guest house, even if it was just temporary, until ChaCha's government connection got them their citizenship. The two were marked for death. If they returned to Colombia, they were dead. Period. Bucks took them in and made sure they were good. They had killed a big dog and his goons in a city that belonged to him, all to protect Bucks.

When Julie tried to refuse them from living with them, Bucks put his foot down, gave her a smack on the ass, then cooked for all of them, so they could all sit and dine together. Then Bucks put it on his woman so good that she passed out with a smile on her face, waking up late the following day with no worries about another woman. Bucks was hers, and at the end of the day, she knew it wholeheartedly.

***

"What up, Pao'?" Bucks asked.

"There is a police at tu puerta," she told him, looking worried.

"It's fine, Paola. He's my boss," Julie said.

Paola blew out a sigh of relief. She nodded her head and walked off.

Bucks helped his woman up off the bed. Julie put a thick fluffy robe on, then with Jarvis Jr., they went to greet their visitor.

***

"Is there a problem, Officer?" Julie joked, after Bucks opened the door.

Ranger's tail wagged excitedly when the Belgian Malinois saw Jarvis Jr. up in Bucks' arms. He set the pup down and let them do what excited dogs did. Lieutenant Sikes stood in a plaid button-up shirt, Wrangler jeans, and work boots, looking like a carpenter instead of a go-hard state trooper.

"Yes, there is a problem, Sergeant Tran. I still haven't received word of a wedding date, so I felt it was my duty to come swing by and see what the holdup is?"

"Weeeell…" Julie paused and looked at Bucks with a smile. "I figure, what would be better than to get married on the day everyone gets together and stuffs their faces?"

"Wow. On Thanksgiving? Now that's original. Who, uh, is gonna be the best man?" Sikes asked, with a hopeful tone in his voice looking at Bucks.

"I was kind of hopin' that you could be that, Sikes," Bucks said.

"You bet your ass I can be! I'd be honored, dude! Fuck yeah, man!" Geeked, Sikes dapped and embraced Bucks like their lives weren't on two different sides of the line.

"Anything on Webster yet? Or his bitch?" Julie asked then.

Sikes shook his head. "No, I'd say they flew the coop, but we thought that last time, and that turned out to be a big mistake. So, all I can say is keep your eyes open. Do not leave without a gun."

Bucks and Julie both nodded.

"Where's T.G. at?" Sikes then asked.

The very sound of his name made Bucks' nostrils flare up. He gritted his teeth in anger, very much still upset about having to let the snake go. Julie had not wanted to allow T.G. to be let go, but then ChaCha explained that releasing the snake was the only way to catch the rat.

"Hunting," Bucks told Sikes.

The lieutenant nodded. He need not hear more.

"I'm ready when I'm needed. Give me a holler, and I'm on the way," he told them.

They nodded their heads.

Embracing Bucks, then hugging Julie, Sikes called his K9 and headed to where his restored 1970 Chevy Nova was parked at the end of the driveway of the mansion.

"He no is immigration?" Bucks and Julie heard asked behind them as Jarvis Jr. came back to them. They turned and saw Viola and Paola at the door, looking worried still.

"No, he's a state trooper, he couldn't care less about getting two ladies that saved my life, so I could save my woman's life, deported."

"Uh, bae...I am the one that saved you," Julie said. "You was locked in a dungeon, I opened the door and let cho' ass out."

Bucks twisted his lip up as the Colombians giggled at the feisty Asian beauty.

"You got it, baby. As long as you—"

BOOM!

The blast instantly stopped Bucks mid-sentence. The ground beneath them shook. Debris from the explosion flew everywhere. Out of instinct, Bucks grabbed his woman and pulled her behind him with Paola and Viola. They all looked towards the end of the driveway and saw Lieutenant Sikes' old school muscle car was now a ball of fire.

"Siiikes! Oh, my Gooood!" Julie screamed as it dawned on her, all in a total of two seconds, Sikes and Ranger were gone.

Paola and Viola started freaking out and hyperventilating. Bucks was stuck, not even sure if what he was seeing was real. Then the sounds of buzzing caught his attention. They all looked up and saw a big hover drone, high up in the air, right over the burning car, facing in their direction.

***

Webster laughed his ass off as he saw Julie, Bucks and two candy-haired Colombian women standing there in the front of the porch of the grand home. He saw the state police sergeant crying her eyes out over the death of Lieutenant Sikes. Her fiancé was so stuck since Webster had utilized his killer remote drone to blow up Sikes' Nova, since he and the dog that had attacked him when he and his dead team managed to abduct Bucks, T.G. and Benicio, got inside the car, he hadn't moved an inch. And the Bogota girls looked like they were in need of a change of underwear.

"You thought shit was sweet, eh?" Webster said to the live video feed, watching them hurry into the house once they peeped the drone. "Think again. I will not rest until all of you are dead and gone. Now I'm gonna' go fuck your little friend in her ass again, while you all lose sleep, scared to death about where and who will be the next one to experience such pain before you take your last breath." He busted out laughing again. "Wow. I should audition to be in a Stephen King movie. That was some twisted shit I just said."

He got behind the wheel of his low-key Chevy Aveo and went to where he landed his drone. He hopped out to grab it, then taking a second look at the burning car, he smirked at it. Jumping back in his tiny little vehicle, Webster pulled off, with nothing else on his mind but getting him some more Yvette, yearning to make her scream again.

Chapter 16

The remainder of her day was okay, for the most part, but Denise was still on edge about the photo. At a meeting with the office staff for the business, Patrice had stuck close to her side, while Charlise stayed by Denise's other side. Nobody else knew about the unspoken threat. Unbeknownst to Denise, Charlise had vowed to her cousin to keep Denise and Letoya safe. She was from the gutter and never feared combat. There was no point in fearing anything. Life was a battle within itself, so Charlise lived by the motto, "Fuck Fear."

***

As nightfall fell upon the A, everyone wrapped it up for the day, with plans for expansion in the future keeping smiles on their faces. They all headed to their cars after bidding adieu to the new boss, and the darling little girl. Denise pushed the stroller towards her Maybach, when Charlise and Patrice pulled up on her in their luxury SUVs.

"Uh-uh, girl. Yo' ass can forget about gettin' in that car 'n rollin' out on yo' own," Charlise declared, getting out of her limited-edition Mercedes G65 AMG and opening the rear driver's side door for her. "In you and the young one goes, Come on."

"Yeah, 'Nise. Whoever this lady is, she sound like she ain't no—"

BOCKA!

"Aaaggghhh!" Patrice screamed when a bullet fired from somewhere flew through her windshield and hit her in her left breast, blowing it to pieces.

"Shit! Get in, Denise!" Charlise urged, grabbing Letoya and hurrying to hand her up to Denise.

BOCKA! BOCKA!

Two more shots came through the windshield of Patrice's Porsche Cayenne Turbo, one slamming into her forehead, blowing her whole upper head off.

Charlise slammed the back door shut and reached for the driver's door.

BOCKA! BOCKA! BOCKA! BOCKA!

Her hand exploded a second before the second slug hit her in the shoulder, slamming her up against the G-Wagon. Denise screamed in fear, holding her crying infant as Charlise took shot after shot until one final one blew her entire head off and splattered her brains all over the rear window, inches away from Denise's face.

"Oh, my God! Oh, my God! Oh, my God! Oh, my Gooood! We're gonna die!" she panicked, terrified.

She was alone and unarmed, with her tiny child. She saw no escape. Charlise had the key fob to the push-start equipped SUV. Denise was too scared to move, much less open the door to grab it. The gunshots stopped. All went silent. Denise cradled her crying baby, holding her close to her. "Shhh! It's okay, baby! We're okay!" Denise cried, looking all around, but barely able to see out the tinted windows, out to the dark parking lot. The rear window exploded just then. Denise jumped out of her skin. The rear passenger window then shattered, then the front, the windshield, and the driver's side windows exploded.

Denise shielded Letoya from the glass shards. A few seconds later, all went silent again. Denise tugged on the door handle to get out. She was a sitting duck if she stayed there any longer. She had a baby to protect, even if that meant giving her own life up to do it. She got the door open and hopped out. She took one step in the direction of her car, her feet in a puddle of Charlise's blood, when she heard the very voice that she dreaded just then.

"One more step, and your legs get shot off, you little bitch!"

Denise's blood ran cold when she felt the barrel of a gun touch the back of her head.

***

Samantha thumbed the hammer of her massive Smith & Wesson 610 revolver, then wrapped her finger around the trigger, gripping it with two hands.

"Normally, I'd give a little speech and a threat before I kill, but fuck all of that! I'm gonna' do what I should have done myself!" she declared through clenched teeth.

"Fuck you and that bastard bitch!"

***

Letoya wailed loudly against her mother's bosom. Denise's tears fell down her face. Her heart beating so fast that it felt like it would explode. She tightened her grip around her daughter and prepared to die. "I love you, Letoya," Denise cried.

"Aaggghhh!"

Denise heard Samantha scream just then. She absentmindedly jumped away as the screams turned to gagging like sounds. She turned around to see Samantha standing there still, but the big revolver was no longer in her hands.

Sticking out of her chest was the blade of a sword covered in her blood. Samantha's light blue shirt had a red stain that grew rapidly. Blood seeped out from the sides of her lips. Her eyes were wide with horror. Denise was dumbfounded. She looked from the blade and saw the tall figure that was standing behind Samantha. She gasped in shock when she realized who had just saved her life…again.

"It…it's you," Denise wept, right before her emotions broke loose.

***

T.G. yanked the sword out of Samantha.

"Close yo' your eyes, Denise!" he told the young mother, then he swung the vintage slicer at Samantha's head, right as she began to fall to her knees. The blade sliced right through the middle of her head, severing it. T.G. swung again, cutting down into Samantha's right shoulder, taking her entire arm off. Her body hit the ground. Blood spurted from the neck stump and where her arm had been. T.G. stared at the dead agent for a minute, half expecting her to jump right back up and get to karate chopping him.

"T-T-Tremaine!" he heard Denise whimper.

He came out of his trance and looked at her. Seeing the precious belle, and hearing the beautiful baby girl crying, the frenzied anger instantly subsided from his heart. He dropped the sword and went to her, wrapping Denise and Letoya in his arms as they both cried.

"I'm here, baby. I got chu'," T.G. told her, holding onto them as if they would both vanish if he let loose even just a little.

"Please! Tell me it's over, Tremaine, baby!" Denise begged, dying to get back to a normal life.

"Almost," T.G. told her. He let them go and ran to the dead agent. He patted the pockets of her cargo pants and felt it in her right pocket. He put his hand in it and pulled Samantha's phone out. "Almost," he then repeated to himself.

He grabbed Denise by her hand and hurried her and Letoya out of the lot, to the street, where his blacked-out 1982 Ford Bronco sat in the darkness, five cars behind the black Lincoln LS that Samantha had hopped out of with a sniper rifle. He got the girls up inside the rammer, started the engine and slamming it into drive, he mashed the gas and got ghost, with nothing but Interstate 75 north in his mind.

***

"Alrighty then, my sweet, beautiful chocolate treat. We're outta here. Next stop, Havana, where nobody will ever find us. "

Webster closed the trunk of the old Dodge Neon after blowing the tied-up Yvette a kiss. He got behind the wheel and pulled off, leaving the old house in the woods of northern Wisconsin's Oneida town. He shot south down to Milwaukee, to where he kept a stash house filled with funds for a rainy day. Fast and in a hurry, Webster ran inside, retrieved the bags filled with cash, totaling in the amount of two point eight million dollars that he had pilfered from drug dealers over the last year.

Tossing them into the back, he got back behind the wheel and make his way to the privately owned airport down in Racine, where under a fake name, he had chartered a flight to get him and his captive out of the country…forever.

***

Arriving at the strip, Webster pulled up to the security booth. Inside, a gorgeous woman, with the brightest red hair and milky-white skin sat. She smiled warmly at him with her sparkling brown cycs.

"Good morning, sir. Flying out today?" she asked in a pleasant manner.

"Indeed, I am. Care to join me, gorgeous?" Webster asked, lusting for the big-breasted belle, desiring to know how her glossy red lips would feel wrapped around his cock.

She giggled. "Aw, that's sweet of you to offer, but I'm a married woman, sir."

Webster chuckled as he handed her his fake ID and his flight itinerary.

"I'm married, too, my wife's in the trunk," he laughed. "No harm, no foul, and what they don't know can't hurt them, right?"

"Not sure I can agree but, if you're looking for fun like that," she said, looking at his ID and his fight manifest. "There are plenty of women where you are going that live for that."

"Sounds great." Webster smiled and thanked her as she handed him his things back. "Maybe I'll see you when I come back for a visit, huh?"

"Hmmmm. I very much doubt you'll ever see me again, Mr. Winston." She gave him another smile with a wink. "Have a great trip, sir."

***

Webster entered and made his way to the hangar where the Learjet he and his prisoner were soon to fly off into the air and disappear from everyone searching high and low for them. The jet was awaiting his arrival. A flight crew of four, the main pilot, the co-pilot, and two flight attendants stood in a line next to the jet's lowered staircase.

"Holy shit! It's got to be my lucky day!" Webster exclaimed, seeing that all four were beautiful women. The pilots were in pants uniforms that seemed to be made to accentuate curvy women and had heels on. The two others were in uniforms with short skirts, pantyhose, and heels. He noticed that the two pilots were tall as hell, one in particular with frosty blue hair that matched her eyes. The one next to her was much shorter and had an hourglass shape that made Webster's eyes go wide. The flight attendants were short and thick. Webster bit his lip as instant visuals of them all naked, getting it in, joining the mile-high club.

***

He pulled the Neon up and parked close to the line of uniformed air models. Hopping out, the two attendants walked up to him with smiles on their faces.

"Hello, Agent Winston. I am Ava, and this is Karlie. Welcome to Sun Rise Air," said the chick with skin the color of pancake syrup, with a femininely raspy voice that added to her undeniable beauty.

"Thank you, Ava. Glad to meet you and Karlie," Webster replied, grabbing the bags of cash from the back row.

"You are said to be escorting a woman to Cuba for facing charges?" Webster heard the woman that had a Middle Eastern look to her, with a voluptuous shape as well, speaking with a heavy Arabic accent.

"Yes, ma'am, she a very dangerous woman."

"Will she be arriving by prison transport team? I do not see her, sir."

"I have her. See, she likes to run, so I had no choice but to subdue her. She's in my trunk," Webster informed her.

"She must be very dangerous," chuckled Ava. "Would you like us to assist with her, or just get your luggage loaded?"

"Uh…I can handle her." Webster looked at the two ladies. "I'll carry my bags, too."

"Good, sir. We are ready to board now," Karlie said to him with a nod.

Webster went to the trunk. He set the bags of money on the ground and took his keys out. Inserting the key into the trunk's keyhole, Webster was suddenly hit with a weird feeling. He looked up and saw the ladies all looking in his way, no longer looking like happy models.

***

Fuck...he's gonna' run! ChaCha thought as she peeped the way Webster was looking at her, Yessy, G-Baby, and Vanessa. Indeed, he did. He yanked the key from the trunk and grabbed his bags to run.

"Agarra 'ese cabrón!" Yessy yelled, upping the Glock 17 she had tucked in the waistline of her uniform pants.

G-Baby and ChaCha's younger cousin upped the 9mm Smith & Wesson, while ChaCha ran to the Neon. The ladies started firing at Webster. Bullets hit the bags of money, exploding them, making the cash fly all over.

ChaCha hurried to pop the trunk and ran to open it. As the shots continued, ChaCha looked inside and saw her tied at her ankles and wrists, barely clothed, looking like she had lost some serious weight from malnourishment.

"Yvette! Ay, Dios Mio!" ChaCha cried, seeing a shell of whom she remembered to be one of the livest women she had ever had the pleasure to meet. She reached in and carefully pulled the half-conscious Yvette from the trunk and hurried her over to where Yessy, G-Baby, and Vanessa were still dumping at Webster, shooting at his feet, making him run in the direction they wanted him to go. They ceased fire when he bent the corner of the hangar and disappeared from their sight.

"Rot in hell, punk-ass piece of caca," Yessy said aloud, anxious for the end result to come.

***

"Son of a bitch! Son of a motherfucking bitch! Who the hell were those bitches?" Webster frantically wondered, as he ran for his life, without his money and without Yvette. At the back of the hangar, he saw an old early 90s Corvette, a late 80s Camaro IROC-Z, and a 1997 Dodge Viper GTS, parked next to each other. Webster hurried to check the cars for keys. When he got inside of the Viper, he discovered the keys were in the ignition. He turned the key and shouted excitedly when the powerful V10 engine started up.

"Yes!"

Webster clutched the stick-shift transmission into gear and peeled off, leaving rubber on the pavement, and smoke behind him. He swerved around the corner where the jet and the lady shooters had been. He saw the blue haired woman putting Yvette inside a Cadillac truck that had not been there minutes ago. The others just stared as he flew by them. Webster rolled the window down and shouted, "You're all dead!" at them.

He saw that not a single one of them moved, nor raised their guns to shoot. He turned back towards the windshield then and yelped in panic when a semi suddenly pulled out in front of him, blocking his path.

"Shit!" he cursed, slamming on the brakes, skidding to a stop just inches from hitting the old rusty-looking trailer. He went to shift into reverse, when the car's engine cut off. "What the fuck?"

Webster tried to start the engine again, but it refused to crank over. He went to get out of the car, but the doors locked and the window rolled back up. Webster then heard the sounds of a helicopter. He leaned forward and looked up out of the windshield. He saw the hovering aircraft right above him.

A loud thump came right above his head. Panicking, Webster started trying to kick out the driver's door window, but it would not break.

"Goddammit!" he yelled angrily, feeling like a rat caught in a trap. He peeped movement in his left peripheral right then. Looking left, he saw the faces of whom he knew were the Valdez family goons. They all had AK-47s, locked, loaded, ready to end him. Then he saw who he had not expected to ever see standing side by side, ever again.

***

Bucks and T.G. gripped their choppers and gritted their teeth as they saw the white man in the Viper looking at them with shock in his eyes.

"Deuces, bitch," T.G. said, raising his AK.

Bucks raised his, then Javi, Macho, Tool, Danny, Xavier, and Evelyn. They all heard Webster scream, right before they all pulled the triggers and opened fire, sending hundreds of rounds at the Viper.

Neither of them stopped shooting until all one hundred rounds of their drums were empty. When they ceased fire, the Viper had more holes in it than a dope head's false explanation. Inside looked like raw meat had been put into a blender and splattered all over. For a minute, Bucks, and T.G. looked at the destroyed supercar. They halfway weren't even convinced that they had finally got him, that they had finally killed Dale Webster. Both letting out sighs of relief, Bucks and T.G. lowered their smoking guns and took it all in. They had him. They had finally won.

Webster was dead, Samantha was dead. The heat was all on the two. Bucks, T.G., Yvette and Julie, were in the clear.

"Bucks?" T.G. spoke just then.

"What, nigga?" Bucks shot back, not even acknowledging him by looking at him.

"I'm sorry, bro. I swear to God, man, I'm sorry."

Bucks shook his head. "You have five seconds to leave, before you end up lookin' like dude, Joe."

The others all stood silently. The only sound was of the helicopter, still hovering high up over the Viper, with a steel cable connected to a powerful magnet descended down on the roof of the Viper. T.G. did as warned. He quick stepped away, not missing a single one of the many mean mugs he had gotten as he hurried to get back to his Bronco. Macho pulled out a two-way radio and spoke into it.

172

"Llevatalo, mujeres," he said to the women that were inside of the Sikorsky.

The Dodge Viper was lifted up from the ground, pieces of it falling off as the helicopter raised it up and hovered it over the open-topped, car-crushing trailer. The helicopter pilot expertly lowered the Viper inside, then detached the magnet from it. It flew off, disappearing from the airport's airspace in less than a minute.

"Care to do the honors, bro?" Macho asked Bucks as he pulled a small key fob remote from the side of his fatigue-print cargo pants. Bucks took the remote. He pressed the green button. The car crusher came to life and crushed the car, smashing and squashing it, until it was a block of scrap metal the size of a schoolteacher's desk.

"Take it to the hot tub!" Macho yelled to the driver then.

The woman behind the wheel of the tractor-trailer gave a thumbs up, then she rolled off, tooting the air horn at her bosses.

Bucks took another deep breath, and watched the big rig bend the corner of the hangar.

"It's over, my nig'," said Javi, patting his back. "Time to go back to yo' woman and turn her into yo' wife, fam."

Bucks nodded his head. "Thank you. All of you, thank you for everything. I really wouldn't have gotten nowhere near this point without help."

"We family, Bucks," Danny said. "No matter what, yo, we ride for family."

"Period," added Tool. "Now if I'm right, we have a couple days before Miss Tran become, Mrs. Tran-Hernz, so let's put all this bullshit behind us and get ready to see the two of y'all tie the knot and complete each other forever."

"Here-here, Joe!" Javi shouted. "And after that, my nigga, we finna' turn thee fuck up!"

Epilogue

Seven Months Later...

"Oh my Gooood, she's so cuuuute!"

"Say thank you, Auntie 'Vette!" Julie cooed, holding her hour's old daughter in her arms in the bed of her room in the maternity ward.

Holding the iPhone up so Yvette could see Julie and the baby via video, Bucks smiled at the picture of his beautiful wife, and their brand-new child. He was filled with glee. He was a husband, a father, rich as shit, and connected like no one would believe.

Julie saw Yvette's eyes fill with tears. It made her own well up.

"Come on, girl, you gon' make me cry if yo' ass get to cryin' again," Julie said. "Ain't that right, Bonita," she added, before kissing her baby's head.

"Ugh. Don't be tryna' turn my niece against me before she even dirties her first diaper. I'll beat cho' Mexican ass."

Julie laughed, as did Bucks.

"Wait 'til I lose this baby fat, I'ma beat both y'all asses," Julie said.

"Yvette, how long 'til you get back, fam? We was hopin you'd be here when Bonita came," Bucks said.

"I know. I'm sorry, boo," Yvette sighed. "I won't be too much longer, though. I been on this job for a while, I have to see it through, you know?"

Bucks turned the camera to face him. "Where you at?"

"That's classified." Yvette chuckled at the face he made. "Stop screw-facin', nigga. I'll be back soon. I'm dyin' to see my niece."

Bucks nodded his head. "Be careful, Yvette."

"I will. I love y'all," she replied.

"We love you, too, babe!" Julie hollered.

The screen went blank when Yvette ended the call. Bucks set the phone down and looked at his family.

"I know Jarvis Jr. gon' be excited as hell when he meets Bonita," he said to his wife.

Julie smiled brightly at her husband. Her heart was filled with joy and peace. She had her family. All the money and status in the world meant not even an eighth as much as her daughter and her husband meant to her. Life was good, and with the plans they had made to turn their names into Jay-Z and Beyoncé worthy brands that even Oprah would shout out to them about, life for Bucks, Julie, and Bonita Hernz would become the epitome of excellence. All they needed was for Yvette to come back, so she could get in where she fit in, and count all the millions of dollars they were going to being in faster than Donald Trump could make up another lie.

***

Yvette sighed to herself, sitting on the bed in her hotel room. She was beyond happy for Bucks and Julie, being reunited and welcoming their child into the world, healthy and strong. But as happy as she was, she was filled with sorrow and forlorn. She and Julie once swore that they would both get married and have children at the same time. It almost brought tears to her eyes, just thinking about it.

"Bitch ass nigga ruined everything," she said to herself, as his face invaded her mind.

Yvette grinded her teeth in anger. Her blood started to boil. In seconds, she grew so irate that she started sweating. Getting up off the bed, she prepared herself to go on the last job she planned on doing. After it was done, she was going to become a normal woman, join forces and finances with Julie and Bucks, and if the Man above was willing, she would meet the man that would really be her king, and build an empire with her that would be handed down to their children, grandchildren, great grandchildren and so on.

***

As the sun began to set, T.G. held onto his fiancée's waist, his hands cupping her big baby bump, while his crotch was pressed against her so-much-phatter ass.

"I have never seen a more beautiful sight, bae," said Denise, holding onto his hands, enjoying the beautiful sunset on the upper terrace of the luxurious grand suite in their hotel.

The beach of Punta Cana was the most relaxing and exotic place that Denise had ever been. She jumped at the chance when T.G. told her that he wanted to take her and Letoya to the Dominican Republic. They packed their bags and shot straight from the estate down in North Miami, to paradise. With no plans on returning anytime soon, T.G. was only thinking about where to next.

"I'm gettin' tired, bae. Wanna call it a day?" Denise asked him.

"Yeah. We got a big day ahead, so we should definitely get some rest."

They stepped back into their suite and headed to their lavish bedroom. Letoya was curled up with her Baby Shark doll sleeping soundly in the big bed.

"Oh, bae, can you bring me a water from the fridge? I need to take my pills," Denise told T.G.

"Yes, my love." He kissed her lips and left her in the bedroom to get her a Fiji water, and a cold beer for himself.

***

In the kitchen, T.G. got a water and Presidente out of the refrigerator, then closed the door. He took a step towards the living area, when his eyes fell upon a brown-skinned woman wearing dark shades, an obvious blonde wig, and a black catsuit with Nike running shoes on her feet. In her right hand she had a .40, with a silencer screwed into the barrel. T.G. took a deep breath, then exhaled. He looked at her. She looked at him. No words were needed to be spoken. Karma was a bitch, and T.G. knew it.

"Guess there ain't no point of me sayin' I have a kid on the way and I'm gettin' married, huh?" he asked her.

Yvette shook her head. "Nope," was her only reply, before she raised her cannon and fired.

PFFT! PFFT! PFFT! PFFT! PFFT!

She emptied the thirteen-round clip into T.G. He flew back against the bloody wall, then slid to the floor bleeding through thirteen big holes. Yvette looked at him for a minute. His eyes closed, then his head dropped. T.G. was gone.

"Now, it's over. Bitch ass nigga," she said to the dead man she had once loved more than she had loved herself.

No sooner than she spat the anger laced words at T.G., a hand suddenly grabbed her by her hair. Her head was yanked back hard. She screamed then she felt her throat opening up, as a razor-sharp blade slid across it. Blood squirted out. She grasped at her throat, trying to hold it in, but it pushed through her fingers. She turned, feeling faint already from the rapid blood loss.

Standing a few feet away, was the soon-to-be mother, woman of her ex-lover, with the bloody knife in her hands, and tears in her eyes.

"Y-y-you bi-bitch!" Yvette stammered to say as she grew so weak that she fell to one knee. Looking up at her, Yvette locked eyes with Denise. She was shocked, angry, and scared all at the same time. She hadn't seen it coming. All she had been focused on was getting her revenge.

Denise then raised the bloody steak knife, screamed and charged at Yvette. Yvette closed her eyes, let her throat go and prepared to go out like a fearless warrior. Then the sting of it came... and that was it.

***

"Aagghh! Nooo!"

Yvette shot up from the bed, grabbing the pistol she had under her pillow. She waved it around, looking for the bitch, but nobody was in front of her with a bloody knife. The door to her bedroom burst open just then. In ran Bucks with a Draco, followed by Jarvis Jr, his minutes-younger sister Eva that replaced the void in Yvette's life from the loss of Sir, and Julie with two MAC 11s.

"Yvette! Hey!" Bucks and Julie ran to her side, while the two puppy dogs tried and failed to jump up on the bed.

"What happened, Yvette? Talk to me!" Julie pleaded, as she sat her gun down and calmly took her cannon out of Yvette's hand.

"I...I th-thought I got him," Yvette wept. "I dreamed I finally killed that bitch ass nigga, JuJu!"

Julie sighed. Her heart broke for Yvette. She knew more than anyone else that Yvette lost sleep over how badly she still wanted T.G.'s head.

Bucks knew, too, but he knew something that Yvette didn't...yet.

He pulled out his iPhone and went into his video archives. Selecting one, he pressed on it.

"I got something for you, lil' momma," Buck told Yvette. "But after you see this, y'all both gotta let go, and go back to being the two bad bitches wit' gunz that niggas knew you and JuJu to be. Okay?"

Yvette looked at him, curious as to what he was about to show her.

Bucks hit play and gave her the phone. Julie sat next to Yvette and watched with her, though she had already seen it when Javi sent it, just minutes before they heard Yvette screaming. The video started playing. On the screen, Yvette saw T.G. hanging upside down by a chair tied around his ankles. She furrowed her eyebrows, then saw he was hanging over dark murky water in what looked like a reptile exhibit at a zoo or something.

Duct tape was over his mouth, muffling his screaming and pleading. His wrists were tied. Wearing only a pair of boxer briefs, Yvette could see blood dripping from what looked like a bunch of puncture wounds all over him. Then seconds later, the surface of the dark water exploded, and shooting up out of it, was a massive crocodile. Yvette gasped in shock when it opened its huge mouth, then snapped it closed, with T.G.'s head inside of it.

The gigantic man-eating carnivore then fell, ripping T.G.'s head and upper half clean off. It slammed back down into the water and devoured its lunch.

"Rest easy now, Yvette," she then heard Javi say. "Him gone, and him will never come back."

The video ended. Yvette took a deep breath, then when she blew it out, she released every negative thing that T.G. had done to her.

"You good, baby?" Julie asked, hugging Yvette in her arms.

"Yeah, I'm good, JuJu."

"Good," said Bucks. "Because now that dude is 'gator food, we're all movin' on, and we about to get richer than we already are. So, we need to be on point and focused. He ain't gon' be the only bitch ass nigga that seems true but ends up tryna' snake us."

"As long as we got us, though," Julie then said, "and our family, everyone else can suck a dirty dick and choke on it. Fuck every hater, every snake, and every trick-ass bitch that's out there!"

"And fuck Donald Trump!" Yvette added. "With his bitch ass! Fuckin' cracker!"

Julie and Bucks busted out laughing at Yvette, then they both hugged and embraced her, reminding her that no matter what, it was the three of them, against the whole world…and Donald Trump.

The End

Lock Down Publications and Ca$h Presents
Assisted Publishing Packages

Due to an increase in the price of services we have increased our prices. The prices below reflect the price increase as of 11/1/24.

BASIC PACKAGE $699 Editing Cover Design Formatting	UPGRADED PACKAGE $1000 Typing Editing Cover Design Formatting Upload eBooks to Amazon Upload Paperback to Amazon
ADVANCE PACKAGE $1,400 Typing Editing (line editing/content) Cover Design Formatting Copyright Registration Proofreading Upload eBooks to Amazon Upload Paperback to Amazon	LDP SUPREME PACKAGE $1,700 Typing Editing (line editing/content) Cover Design Formatting Copyright Registration Proofreading Set up Amazon Account Upload eBooks to Amazon Upload Paperback to Amazon Advertise on LDP's Amazon and Facebook Page

***

Other services available upon request.
Additional charges may apply

Lock Down Publications
P.O. Box 944
Stockbridge, GA 30281-9998
Phone: 470 303-9761
Email: lockdownpublications@gmail.com

Submission Guideline

Submit the first three chapters of your completed manuscript to ldpsubmissions@gmail.com. In the subject line add **Your Book's Title**. The manuscript must be in a Word Doc file and sent as an attachment. Document should be in Times New Roman, double spaced, and in size 12 font. Also, provide your synopsis and full contact information. If sending multiple submissions, they must each be in a separate email.

Have a story but no way to send it electronically? You can still submit to LDP/Ca$h Presents. Send in the first three chapters, written or typed, of your completed manuscript to:

LDP: Submissions Dept
P.O. Box 944
Stockbridge, GA 30281-9998

DO NOT send original manuscript. Must be a duplicate. Provide your synopsis and a cover letter containing your full contact information.

Thanks for considering LDP and Ca$h Presents.

NEW RELEASES

BLOODLINE OF A SAVAGE 1-3
THESE VICIOUS STREETS 1-3
RELENTLESS GOON 1-3
BY PRINCE A. TAUHID

THE BUTTERFLY MAFIA 1-3
BY FUMIYA PAYNE

A THUG'S STREET PRINCESS 1&2
BY MEESHA

CITY OF SMOKE 3
BY MOLOTTI

GET IT IN SLUGS 1 &2
BY B. STALL

STANDING ON HER BUSINESS 1&2
BY DG SANTANA

STEPPERS 1,2&3
THE REAL BADDIES OF CHI-RAQ
BY KING RIO

THE LANE 1&2
BY KEN-KEN SPENCE

THUG OF SPADES 1&2
LOVE IN THE TRENCHES 2
CORNER BOYS
BY COREY ROBINSON

TIL DEATH 3
BY ARYANNA

CHRISTOPHER "DIESEL" HORNEZES

THE BIRTH OF A GANGSTER 4
BY DELMONT PLAYER

PRODUCT OF THE STREETS 1-3
BY DEMOND "MONEY" ANDERSON

NO TIME FOR ERROR
BY KEESE

MONEY HUNGRY DEMONS 1-2
BY TRANAY ADAMS

HUB CITY MENACE 1-3
BY J. WHITE

A THUGGISH PASSION 1&2
LAND OF DA HOOLIGANZ 1-4
KILLAZ ON STANDBY 1&2
BY IRA B.

FO'EVA ROLLIN 1&2
BY ASSA RAYMOND BAKER

THE LEVEL UP 1&3
BY LUXURY KING

Coming Soon from Lock Down Publications/Ca$h Presents

IF YOU CROSS ME ONCE 6
ANGEL V
By Anthony Fields

A THUGS STREET PRINCESS 3
By Meesha

CORNER BOYS 2
By Corey Robinson

THA TAKEOVER
By Keith Chandler

BETRAYAL OF A G 2
By Ray Vinci

SAVAGE FAMILY EMPIRE 1&2
SOULLESS GOON 1,2&3
THE DIRTY SIDE OF MONEY 1,2&3
By Prince

FOR MY ENEMY'S SAKE
AMBITIONS OF A SLIDER
FRESH OFF DA PORCH
By IRA B.

THE TRUCKLOAD 1-4
TIPPIN' THE SCALES 1-3
BAD BITCHES WIT GUNZ 3
PROBLEM SOLVED 2
By Christopher "Diesel" Hornezes

CHRISTOPHER "DIESEL" HORNEZES

Available Now

RESTRAINING ORDER 1 & 2
By **CA$H & Coffee**

LOVE KNOWS NO BOUNDARIES 1-3
By **Coffee**

RAISED AS A GOON I, II, III & IV
BRED BY THE SLUMS I, II, III
BLAST FOR ME I & II
ROTTEN TO THE CORE I II III
A BRONX TALE I, II, III
DUFFLE BAG CARTEL I II III IV V VI
HEARTLESS GOON I II III IV V
A SAVAGE DOPEBOY I II
DRUG LORDS I II III
CUTTHROAT MAFIA I II
KING OF THE TRENCHES
By **Ghost**

LAY IT DOWN I & II
LAST OF A DYING BREED I II
BLOOD STAINS OF A SHOTTA I & II III
By **Jamaica**

LOYAL TO THE GAME I II III
LIFE OF SIN I, II III
By **TJ & Jelissa**

IF LOVING HIM IS WRONG...I & II
LOVE ME EVEN WHEN IT HURTS I II III
By **Jelissa**

PUSH IT TO THE LIMIT
By **Bre' Hayes**

BAD B*TCHES WIT' GUNZ 3

BLOODY COMMAS I & II
SKI MASK CARTEL I, II & III
KING OF NEW YORK I II, III IV V
RISE TO POWER I II III
COKE KINGS I II III IV V
BORN HEARTLESS I II III IV
KING OF THE TRAP I II
By **T.J. Edwards**

WHEN THE STREETS CLAP BACK I & II III
THE HEART OF A SAVAGE I II III IV
MONEY MAFIA I II
LOYAL TO THE SOIL I II III
By **Jibril Williams**

A DISTINGUISHED THUG STOLE MY HEART I II & III
LOVE SHOULDN'T HURT I II III IV
RENEGADE BOYS 1-4
PAID IN KARMA 1-3
SAVAGE STORMS 1-3
AN UNFORESEEN LOVE 1-3
BABY, I'M WINTERTIME COLD 1-3
A THUG'S STREET PRINCESS 1&2
By **Meesha**

A GANGSTER'S CODE 1-3
A GANGSTER'S SYN 1-3
THE SAVAGE LIFE 1-3
CHAINED TO THE STREETS 1-3
BLOOD ON THE MONEY 1-3
A GANGSTA'S PAIN 1-3
BEAUTIFUL LIES AND UGLY TRUTHS
CHURCH IN THESE STREETS
By **J-Blunt**

CUM FOR ME 1-8
An LDP Erotica Collaboration

CHRISTOPHER "DIESEL" HORNEZES

BLOOD OF A BOSS 1-5
SHADOWS OF THE GAME
TRAP BASTARD
By **Askari**

THE STREETS BLEED MURDER 1-3
THE HEART OF A GANGSTA 1-3
By **Jerry Jackson**

WHEN A GOOD GIRL GOES BAD
By **Adrienne**

THE COST OF LOYALTY 1-3
By **Kweli**

BRIDE OF A HUSTLA 1-3
THE FETTI GIRLS 1-3
CORRUPTED BY A GANGSTA 1-4
BLINDED BY HIS LOVE
THE PRICE YOU PAY FOR LOVE 1-3
DOPE GIRL MAGIC 1-3
By **Destiny Skai**

A KINGPIN'S AMBITION
A KINGPIN'S AMBITION II
I MURDER FOR THE DOUGH
By **Ambitious**

TRUE SAVAGE 1-7
DOPE BOY MAGIC 1-3
MIDNIGHT CARTEL 1-3
CITY OF KINGZ 1&2
NIGHTMARE ON SILENT AVE
THE PLUG OF LIL MEXICO 1&2
CLASSIC CITY
By **Chris Green**

BAD B*TCHES WIT' GUNZ 3

A GANGSTER'S REVENGE 1-4
THE BOSS MAN'S DAUGHTERS 1-5
A SAVAGE LOVE 1&2
BAE BELONGS TO ME 1&2
A HUSTLER'S DECEIT 1-3
WHAT BAD BITCHES DO 1-3
SOUL OF A MONSTER 1-3
KILL ZONE
A DOPE BOY'S QUEEN 1-3
TIL DEATH 1-3
IMMA DIE BOUT MINE 1-6
DYING FOR LIKES
By **Aryanna**

A DOPEBOY'S PRAYER
By **Eddie "Wolf" Lee**

THE KING CARTEL 1-3
By **Frank Gresham**

THESE NIGGAS AIN'T LOYAL 1-3
By **Nikki Tee**

GANGSTA SHYT 1-3
By **CATO**

THE ULTIMATE BETRAYAL
By **Phoenix**

BOSS'N UP 1-3
By **Royal Nicole**

I LOVE YOU TO DEATH
By **Destiny J**

I RIDE FOR MY HITTA
I STILL RIDE FOR MY HITTA
By **Misty Holt**

189

CHRISTOPHER "DIESEL" HORNEZES

LOVE & CHASIN' PAPER
By **Qay Crockett**

TO DIE IN VAIN
SINS OF A HUSTLA
By **ASAD**

BROOKLYN HUSTLAZ
By **Boogsy Morina**

BROOKLYN ON LOCK 1 & 2
By **Sonovia**

GANGSTA CITY
By **Teddy Duke**

A DRUG KING AND HIS DIAMOND 1-3
A DOPEMAN'S RICHES
HER MAN, MINE'S TOO 1&2
CASH MONEY HO'S
THE WIFEY I USED TO BE 1&2
PRETTY GIRLS DO NASTY THINGS
By **Nicole Goosby**

LIPSTICK KILLAH 1-3
CRIME OF PASSION 1-3
FRIEND OR FOE 1-3
By **Mimi**

TRAPHOUSE KING 1-3
KINGPIN KILLAZ 1-3
STREET KINGS 1&2
PAID IN BLOOD 1&2
CARTEL KILLAZ 1-3
DOPE GODS 1&2
By **Hood Rich**

THE STREETS ARE CALLING
By **Duquie Wilson**

BAD B*TCHES WIT' GUNZ 3

STEADY MOBBN' 1-3
THE STREETS STAINED MY SOUL 1-3
By **Marcellus Allen**

WHO SHOT YA 1-3
SON OF A DOPE FIEND 1-4
HEAVEN GOT A GHETTO 1&2
SKI MASK MONEY 1&2
By **Renta**

GORILLAZ IN THE BAY 1-4
TEARS OF A GANGSTA 1/&2
3X KRAZY 1&2
STRAIGHT BEAST MODE 1&2
By **DE'KARI**

TRIGGADALE 1-3
MURDA WAS THE CASE 1-3
By **Elijah R. Freeman**

SLAUGHTER GANG 1-3
RUTHLESS HEART 1-3
By **Willie Slaughter**

GOD BLESS THE TRAPPERS 1-3
THESE SCANDALOUS STREETS 1-3
FEAR MY GANGSTA 1-5
THESE STREETS DON'T LOVE NOBODY 1-2
BURY ME A G 1-5
A GANGSTA'S EMPIRE 1-4
THE DOPEMAN'S BODYGAURD 1&2
THE REALEST KILLAZ 1-3
THE LAST OF THE OGS 1-3
By **Tranay Adams**

MARRIED TO A BOSS 1-3
By **Destiny Skai & Chris Green**

CHRISTOPHER "DIESEL" HORNEZES

KINGZ OF THE GAME 1-7
CRIME BOSS 1-4
By **Playa Ray**

FUK SHYT
By **Blakk Diamond**

DON'T F#CK WITH MY HEART 1&2
By **Linnea**

ADDICTED TO THE DRAMA 1-3
IN THE ARM OF HIS BOSS
By **Jamila**

LOYALTY AIN'T PROMISED 1&2
By **Keith Williams**

YAYO 1-4
A SHOOTER'S AMBITION 1&2
BRED IN THE GAME
By **S. Allen**

TRAP GOD 1-3
RICH $AVAGE 1-3
MONEY IN THE GRAVE 1-3
CARTEL MONEY 1&2
By **Martell Troublesome Bolden**

FOREVER GANGSTA 1&2
GLOCKS ON SATIN SHEETS 1&2
By **Adrian Dulan**

TOE TAGZ 1-4
LEVELS TO THIS SHYT 1&2
IT'S JUST ME AND YOU
By **Ah'Million**

BAD B*TCHES WIT' GUNZ 3

KINGPIN DREAMS 1-3
RAN OFF ON DA PLUG
By **Paper Boi Rari**

THE STREETS MADE ME 1-3
By **Larry D. Wright**

CONFESSIONS OF A GANGSTA 1-4
CONFESSIONS OF A JACKBOY 1-3
CONFESSIONS OF A HITMAN
CONFESSIONS OF A DOPE BOY
By **Nicholas Lock**

I'M NOTHING WITHOUT HIS LOVE
SINS OF A THUG
TO THE THUG I LOVED BEFORE
A GANGSTA SAVED XMAS
IN A HUSTLER I TRUST
By **Monet Dragun**

QUIET MONEY 1-3
THUG LIFE 1-3
EXTENDED CLIP 1&2
A GANGSTA'S PARADISE
By **Trai'Quan**

CAUGHT UP IN THE LIFE 1-3
THE STREETS NEVER LET GO 1-3
By **Robert Baptiste**

NEW TO THE GAME 1-3
MONEY, MURDER & MEMORIES 1-3
By **Malik D. Rice**

CREAM 2-3
THE STREETS WILL TALK
By **Yolanda Moore**

CHRISTOPHER "DIESEL" HORNEZES

THE STREETS WILL NEVER CLOSE 1-3
By **K'ajji**

LIFE OF A SAVAGE 1-4
A GANGSTA'S QUR'AN 1-4
MURDA SEASON 1-3
GANGLAND CARTEL 1-3
CHI'RAQ GANGSTAS 1-4
KILLERS ON ELM STREET 1-3
JACK BOYZ N DA BRONX 1-3
A DOPEBOY'S DREAM 1-3
JACK BOYS VS DOPE BOYS 1-3
COKE GIRLZ
COKE BOYS
SOSA GANG 1&2
BRONX SAVAGES
BODYMORE KINGPINS
BLOOD OF A GOON
By **Romell Tukes**

CONCRETE KILLA 1-3
VICIOUS LOYALTY 1-3
BLOODY MONEY BAGS
By **Kingpen**

THE ULTIMATE SACRIFICE 1-6
KHADIFI
IF YOU CROSS ME ONCE 1-3
ANGEL 1-4
IN THE BLINK OF AN EYE
By **Anthony Fields**

THE LIFE OF A HOOD STAR
By **Ca$h & Rashia Wilson**

NIGHTMARES OF A HUSTLA 1-3
BLOOD AND GAMES 1&2
By **King Dream**

BAD B*TCHES WIT' GUNZ 3

GHOST MOB
By **Stilloan Robinson**

HARD AND RUTHLESS 1&2
MOB TOWN 251
THE BILLIONAIRE BENTLEYS 1-3
REAL G'S MOVE IN SILENCE
By **Von Diesel**

MOB TIES 1-7
SOUL OF A HUSTLER, HEART OF A KILLER 1-3
GORILLAZ IN THE TRENCHES
OOPS CRY TOO 1&2
THE DAUGHTER OF A CARTEL BOSS
By **SayNoMore**

BODYMORE MURDERLAND 1-3
THE BIRTH OF A GANGSTER 1-4
By **Delmont Player**

FOR THE LOVE OF A BOSS 1&2
By **C. D. Blue**

KILLA KOUNTY 1-5
TENDER
By **Khufu**

MOBBED UP 1-4
THE BRICK MAN 1-5
THE COCAINE PRINCESS 1-10
STEPPERS 1-3
SUPER GREMLIN 1-4
A GANGSTA'S SON
By **King Rio**

MONEY GAME 1&2
By **Smoove Dolla**

CHRISTOPHER "DIESEL" HORNEZES

A GANGSTA'S KARMA 1-5
By **FLAME**

KING OF THE TRENCHES 1-3
By **GHOST & TRANAY ADAMS**

BAD BITCHES WIT GUNZ 1&2
PROBLEM SOLVED
By "Christopher Diesel" Hornezes

QUEEN OF THE ZOO 1&2
By **Black Migo**

GRIMEY WAYS 1-3
BETRAYAL OF A G
By **Ray Vinci**

XMAS WITH AN ATL SHOOTER
By **Ca$h & Destiny Skai**

KING KILLA 1&2
By **Vincent "Vitto" Holloway**

BETRAYAL OF A THUG 1&2
By **Fre$h**

COUNTDOWN OF A KILLA 1&2
SEX, MURDER AND GOD 1&2
GUNS DOWN, BOTTOMS UP 1&2
By Lo-Life

THE MURDER QUEENS 1-7
By **Michael Gallon**

FOR THE LOVE OF BLOOD 1-4
By **Jamel Mitchell**

BAD B*TCHES WIT' GUNZ 3

HOOD CONSIGLIERE 1&2
NO TIME FOR ERROR
By **Keese**

PROTÉGÉ OF A LEGEND 1,2&3
LOVE IN THE TRENCHES 1&2
By **Corey Robinson**

THE PLUG'S RUTHLESS DAUGHTER 1&2
By **Tony Daniels**

BORN IN THE GRAVE 1-3
CRIME PAYS
By **Self Made Tay**

MOAN IN MY MOUTH
By **XTASY**

TORN BETWEEN A GANGSTER AND A GENTLEMAN
By **J-BLUNT & Miss Kim**

LOYALTY IS EVERYTHING 1-3
CITY OF SMOKE 1-3
By **Molotti**

HERE TODAY GONE TOMORROW 1&2
By **Fly Rock**

WOMEN LIE MEN LIE 1-4
FIFTY SHADES OF SNOW 1-3
STACK BEFORE YOU SPLURGE
GIRLS FALL LIKE DOMINOES
NAÏVE TO THE STREETS
By **ROY MILLIGAN**

PILLOW PRINCESS
By **S. Hawkins**

CHRISTOPHER "DIESEL" HORNEZES

THE BUTTERFLY MAFIA 1-3
SALUTE MY SAVAGERY 1&2
By **Fumiya Payne**

THE LANE 1&2
By Ken-Ken Spence

THE PUSSY TRAP 1-5
By **Nene Capri**

DIRTY DNA
By **Blaque**

SANCTIFIED AND HORNY
by **XTASY**

BOOKS BY LDP'S CEO, CA$H

TRUST IN NO MAN
TRUST IN NO MAN 2
TRUST IN NO MAN 3
BONDED BY BLOOD
SHORTY GOT A THUG
THUGS CRY
THUGS CRY 2
THUGS CRY 3
TRUST NO BITCH
TRUST NO BITCH 2
TRUST NO BITCH 3
TIL MY CASKET DROPS
RESTRAINING ORDER
RESTRAINING ORDER 2
IN LOVE WITH A CONVICT
LIFE OF A HOOD STAR
XMAS WITH AN ATL SHOOTER